Death Stalks Port Severn Locks

by Penny Johnston

Penny Johnston, Publisher

© Copyright 2020 by Penny Johnston

All rights reserved. No part of this publication may be reproduced, stored in a retrieval system, distributed or transmitted, in any form or by any means, electronic, mechanical, photocopying, recording, or otherwise without the prior written permission of the copyright owners. The scanning, uploading and distribution of this book via the Internet, or via any other means, without the permission of the publisher, is illegal and punishable by law. Please purchase only authorized electronic editions, and do not participate in or encourage electronic piracy of copyrighted materials. Your support of the author's rights is appreciated.

Penny Johnston, Publisher

The characters and events in this book are fictitious. Any similarity to real persons, living or dead, is coincidental and not intended by the author.

ISBN: 978-1-716-24148-2

Cover Design by Sara Carrick

Detective and Mystery stories, Canadian (English). Johnston, Penny

Other Mariposa Murder Mysteries by Penny Johnston

Therapy for the Dead (2015)

Frozen lies the Librarian (2016)

Murder at Mass Rock (2018)

Dedicated to the late Lillian Uren, Richard and Wendy Johnston

Acknowledgements

Thank you to Alex Wilmot, editing; Sara Carrick, design and artwork; Ed Adach, Forensics, Toronto Police Service; Robert Barnett, photo.

Chapter 1

It was a warm evening, with not a cloud in the sky. He turned into the driveway and parked his car next to his house, a nice middle- class residence in north Mariposa, then he looked in the mirror and adjusted it so he could check out his face. There was a slight red smudge mark on his cheek, hard to see but not for someone with a discerning eye. His wife had a discerning eye. He reached into the glove compartment for a tissue and wiped it off.

Getting out the first thing he looked at were his rose bushes, which gave him joy their colour, their fragrance and their gentle beauty He loved gardening. He had fertilized the bushes with manure, watered them carefully, and now looked at the results. He walked over to sniff a blossom. It was then that he noticed a man-size sneaker footprint in the black soil next to the front bay window. Someone had been peering into his living room. Someone had been spying on him.

To steal?

He hurried to the front door to check that it was locked. He could hear his phone ringing and hurried inside to answer it.

"You're a dead man walking." It was that caller again with the same message, the same tone of voice. He looked for the caller ID. It was blocked. This had been going on for several months now. This time, he decided to do something about it. He wasn't going to go to the police he was afraid that, as a lawyer he would look foolish. What could the police do? Nothing had happened to him physically. His house hadn't been broken into, only the threatening phone calls, and he didn't have a number to give them. The best plan of action would be to speak to his long-time partner at his law firm, Mel Stone. Mel might have some practical suggestions.

The next morning, he arrived early and knocked on Mel's door. When the door opened Mel looked a bit surprised to see him. "Mel, I have to talk to you, confidentially. Can we take a break this morning? Apple Annie's would be a good place to have our chat," he said.

"Sure thing. I hope it's not something serious. I just have to make a few phone calls, then I can be with you."

Reg bit his lip with impatience.

They walked up the block to Apple Annie's, an interesting coffee shop on Mississauga, the main street. The walls were hung with colourful oils, some of flowers, some portraits done by local artists. It served all kinds of coffee, but Reg opted for black and so did Mel. Once they paid, they took a pine wooden table at the back. The early morning crowd had already drifted in and were claiming the tables at the front.

When they were seated, Mel asked. "What's on your mind? It's not often we have the big discussion." He took a eucalyptus pastille out of his pocket and popped it into his mouth.

"I'll skip the preliminaries. I'm receiving threatening phone calls. It's a man's voice. The caller gives the same message, I'm a dead man walking. It's been going on for several months now. I want it to stop, but I have no idea on how to do that."

"So, you've no idea as to who it is? Or what he's referring to?"

"No. Since going into private practice and taking criminal defense cases, I've made no enemies so far as I can see, no bitter clients over cases that I have lost, and no one has directly complained to me. I keep my fees reasonable. Things have been calm. No one has threatened me or voiced displeasure. But last night, I began thinking about when I was a crown prosecutor, in Barrie at the beginning of my career. Then things were different. I used to get threats."

"Tell me about it," said Mel, leaning forward to catch everything and to show his interest in what his partner had to say.

"I remember one case where the victim was a woman. The accused and his wife had gone on their honeymoon to Niagara Falls. He claimed that they went to a lookout point, surrounded by gorse bushes and trees to get a good look at the Canadian Falls.

"His story was that his wife had tripped on a tree root lost her balance and fallen forward over the guard rail before he could do anything about it before he could grab her. She plunged to her death on the rocks. He claimed it was an accident. But the security fence was waist high and it would have been difficult to go over. He was found guilty of manslaughter by the jury. The crown felt it was murder, a deliberate planned murder. He had taken out life insurance on her several weeks before they got married. His name was let me see, if I've got that right, Terry Falls. Before he was sentenced, he was allowed to say a few words. He shouted out to the court that he was innocent and said that he wouldn't rest until he got even with me.

"That's one I recall. It sticks in my mind. Mel, if you check old newspaper accounts, you'll find several murders committed by either the man or the woman on their honeymoon involving a push over a cliff or over the falls. It's not a very original way to murder your partner."

"Have you any idea what happened to him?" asked Mel

Reg shook his head. "Served his time and then got out, I guess. I don't keep up with the convicted."

"No idea where he is now?" asked Mel

"None at all. I just remember the threat."

"When he was arrested, he kept saying he was innocent, but we had the man and his wife on security camera entering the lookout point and then with him standing right behind her at the fence, and then her fall.

"Another case I handled was more interesting. A couple with a baby, who had Downs syndrome went down to see Niagara Falls on a day sigh-t seeing trip. The wife was standing at a lookout point holding the baby up in her arms. She became dizzy, she said, momentarily losing her balance. In doing so she dropped the baby down into the gorge and the baby died on the rocks below. The police tried to press charges but didn't get anywhere. She had a good lawyer and the police decided that there was no criminal intent and charges were dropped by the Crown. It was labeled an accident.

"Another criminal who threatened me was Joseph Bathe, who again claimed he was innocent and when asked if he had anything to say, screamed at me at the top of his lungs that he was innocent before he was sentenced for his crime. When convicted he got fifteen years. Looking directly at me, he whispered, "I'm going to get you when I get out, no matter how long it takes."

"They all make threats, but do they make good on their threats?" said Mel reflectively. He examined his cufflinks, fourteen carat gold, marveling at how much he paid for them. Then he gave an admiring glance down at his soft Italian made leather shoes, nothing but the best.

Reg didn't skip a beat in his narration. "The Crown alleged that when his wife was taking a bath. Bathe dropped the live radio into her bath. The steel drain in the tub grounded the charge and she was electrocuted. He claimed that he was nowhere near the bathroom. His story was that in reaching the radio to turn it off, her hand slipped, knocking it into the water. Forensics didn't not find her fingerprints on the radio."

Mel said, "That kind of death is always suspicious. The odd case pops up here and there over the years, of a male or female taking a bath and an electric appliance accidentally falls into the water. Never a hair dryer, because they've been built with a ground fault interrupter which turns the current off on hitting the water."

"Well. In this case, it turned out the husband and wife were not getting along. There were many loud fights with the police being called to the home for domestic assault. The wife wanted a divorce, custody of the children, etc. The next thing is that police come to the home and find her electrocuted in the bath. His story was fishy. He was convicted of second-degree murder. He got fifteen years. Spent his time at Warkworth."

"Here let me write down the names on my pad in case we need them. Can you think of anyone else?" asked Mel.

"I recall in my experiences working for the Crown, another popular way to dispose of your spouse or relative is to push them downstairs. Henry Steppes claimed that his wife had gone down the cellar steps to check on some canned preserves on a shelf. She tripped on a loose nail jutting out of a board and fell, hitting her head on the cement floor. Coming home from work, Steppes said he found her unconscious at the bottom of the stairs. She died later in hospital of a hematoma of the brain which was revealed by a CT scan."

"Yeh, I remembered reading about that case," said Mel.

"For the Crown, the big question was, did she trip or was she pushed? We figured out that he was guilty. He was convicted of manslaughter. From the stand, when he was asked if he had anything to say, Harold Steppes swore on the Bible that he would get me, if it was the last thing he did.

"In similar cases that I researched and successfully prosecuted over the years, there were defense wounds on the victim's hands, deep gashes to back of head, plus a big fat insurance policy taken out a week or months before which all screamed guilty,

guilty." Mel nodded his head and took a sip of coffee. He said, "In one case I was reading up on, the son claimed his mother slipped and went over the railing of the staircase. Investigators found that the rail was higher than her centre of gravity. In other words, she was pushed. The son claimed that she was wearing socks and had slipped. Bruises, on her arms showed that she was still alive when she landed, but the back of the eye socket, was broken, by a vicious kick or punch.

"In another case, the wife had acute subdural hematoma, where the brain swells. and bruises on her arms which showed she was alive when she fell. She died of her injuries."

Reg continued, "But in the case of Harold Steppes, on appeal he was granted a new trial. In that new trial, the new evidence showed that the wife had accidentally tripped on the stairs. He was released.

"Mel, I've given it a great deal of thought and those are the three strongest possibilities. All three threatened me in no uncertain terms. It was ten or more years ago, so they could no longer be in jail. Some might be out on probation.

"I think we should give those names to the police and tell them about the threatening phone calls. It may be one of them."

"But why has it taken so long for any of them to make good on their threats? Why now?" questioned Mel. "It's over ten years."

"I don't know. I have been reluctant to go to the police. I didn't want to look foolish and they will say there is nothing they can do without a physical altercation. I can't even get a peace bond."

"A threat is a threat," said Mel. "This person is out to kill you, make no mistake about that. The threats aren't going to stop. You could soon be dead if you don't do something about this."

"Thanks, Mel. I'll go into the OPP office tomorrow."

"Who knows? Tomorrow may be too late."

Chapter 2

At the OPP office, it was a slow morning so far. Few calls. Clancy sat back in his chair biting into a maple dip doughnut while sipping Tim's coffee

But then the phone rang, Clancy picked up the call. It was Judge Wiffy calling from Southwood, his home on the Pellatt estate in north Mariposa. During the night someone had broken into the house and stolen some valuable items. Would they come out right away and investigate?

"Southwood is a well-known palatial home," said David. "Beatrice Hamilton's uncle was Major Henry Pellatt, father of Colonel Henry Pellatt who built Casa Loma in Toronto. Southwood was his home, complete with tennis courts and swimming pool. While playing on the grass tennis courts in 1896, Beatrice met Stephen Leacock. She later became his wife. Even today Southwood is a well-known property."

"My, you are a fountain of information, David. Caught up in local history, are you? You must get it from that pretty schoolteacher, you're hanging around with."

David smiled, but said nothing.

"Let's get right over," said Clancy

A brick house with second storey dormer windows, and an Impressive front door, with portals on either side, the house was situated on a large expanse of lawn sloping down to Lake Couchiching. David and Clancy passed the stone pillars at the entrance of the driveway and drove up the long circular path to the front door.

Clancy glanced up at the bright blue sky and down through

the trees at the lake. It was quiet, no sign of motorboats roaring about. There was the smell of cut grass.

At the front door, they met a very upset Judge Wiffy, a man in his early sixties. Tiny red capillaries popped up on the surface of his nose. Was this from drinking? He had a rotund figure probably from dining at too many banquets He wore an open neck shirt and lounge trousers.

Without further ado, he ushered them straight into the library, located in a wing off the living room.

Books were strewn across the floor, the letters of Winston Churchill, his autobiographies; the letters of Hugh Trevor Roper; the annuals of the Champlain Society were dumped from their shelves in a heap. Desk drawers had been pulled out and the contents dumped on the floor. Papers were lying scattered about on the rug.

"Í was writing my memoirs." said Judge Wiffy. His desk was a mess of papers, a stapler, letter opener, pencil sharpener, stamps, envelopes, fountain pens and pencils. "It will take forever for the cleaning lady to clean this mess up."

Mahogany bookcases lining the walls had had their glass doors pried open, the locks broken by a crude pen knife. That lovely wood so thoughtlessly damaged, thought Clancy. Even the chrome and glass drink cart had been turned over with the bottles and liquids spilling onto the rug.

"My good Scottish malt whisky, aged over twenty years," said the judge, sadly, "you'd think they'd have more respect. Thieves even slashed the green leather sofa."

"How did they get in?" asked Clancy.

The judge pointed to the library door fronting the garden terrace. They looked at the door where the pane of glass had been cut out with a glass cutter and removed opposite,

"Do you have security?"

"I have a camera on the outside. but all I got when I looked at it was a dark figure in hoodie and jeans, scurrying away like the rat he was. Yes, the inside alarm must have been accidentally turned off. The way the thief entered he didn't break the glass, he cut it, then just reached through the glass opening, and turned the door handle. That's why I didn't hear anything," said Judge Wiffy,

"What was taken? What seems to be missing?"

"Most of it was valuable, like hockey memorabilia, a hockey sweater that belong to Jean Belliveau and a gold signet ring with the scales of justice that was given to me, a personal gift. My most prized possession was a first edition of Stephen Leacock's, *Sunshine Sketches of a Little Town,* published in 1912, which I bought for sentimental reasons. I also have the 1913 edition illustrated by graphic artist, Seth. Who would want that? You would have to be a collector to want that."

"We'll check outside on the grounds for footprints around the house. You live alone?" asked Clancy

I have a housekeeper. My wife died a year ago. She comes in daily, does not stay overnight. She wouldn't have been here when the robbery occurred."

"Can you think of anyone?"

"Not off-hand. I'm in a state of shock. There's very little theft in the neighbourhood, probably because we've installed security cameras. I haven't heard of a break- in in a long time."

"Well the first place to look after we've e dusted for prints is outside to see if there is a footprint," said Greg, the third member of their team specializing in break and enter.

"Then we'll look on eBay," said Clancy, "that will be the first place they'll try to unload or Craig's List. We'll check out the neighbourhood bars and pool halls where they usually unload stuff.

"It looks like a pretty sophisticated thief who did this. At first, I thought it might be someone like Jimmy Snipes and his gang, petty drug dealers who steal to finance their habits, but he wouldn't know how to offload the loot. This was a thief who knew what was valuable in your collection and knew that it was there."

"Start with the library door and see what you can find there. He used a cut glass cutter. Here's the pane of glass." Clancy picked up two shards of glass off the rug and held them up to the light. "Crystal clear. He wore gloves."

Turning to the judge, who was obviously in distress, he asked, "Considering the amount of destruction you're sure you didn't hear a thing?"

"Well, I'm hard of hearing."

"Who knows about your collection? What about insurance?"

"Any guest to the house, I suppose. We entertained. I was very proud of my collection. I showed it to my guests. I'm insured, but the things taken are irreplaceable."

"May I speak with your housekeeper? How long has she worked here?"

"Ten years. She is very reliable."

He called Irma out of the kitchen where she was making lunch.

She came along the hall, a fat pleasant woman with a big white apron covering her blue pant suit.

"Have you seen anyone loitering around, parked outside for periods of time watching the house? Anyone who looked like they were casing the building?"

"Well a day or so ago a man in his thirties rang the bell. I didn't answer it. I figured that he was selling real estate or life insurance. I watched him from behind the curtain in the front living room. I saw him sneak around the house peering into the back windows. He had a lot of nerve. He went around to the side, past the library and it was there I lost him."

"Would you describe him to me."

"He was slim, tall about six feet, dark hair, wearing a dark suit, carrying a black leather briefcase. What stuck out was that he was wearing black running shoes, something that I would not expect from a man carrying a brief- case. The running shoes looked out of place."

"Would he be caught on your security camera?"

"It was on a couple of days ago. Let me take you over to it and we'll rewind it."

"There he is." The security camera was grainy and didn't give the best results, but it could help.

"Well Greg, you've got your work cut out for you. The goods will be off loaded quickly in the next few days for ready cash and then the trail will pick up or grow cold. So, let's be quick as we can."

Chapter 3

Back at the office, Clancy sat at his desk and let Greg make out the losses in triplicate. Then the phone rang. A soft woman's voice said. "I wish to report a missing person."

"Who would that be?" asked Clancy, hoping that the caller was not from a seniors' home to report another geriatric with Alzheimer's who had escaped from his long-term care and had gone wandering in the night down Highway 11 to Toronto. There had been a few cases lately. They were a real pain to deal with - searching backyards, sheds and rubbish bins, for wily seniors. The last one they tracked down had wandered up to his old cottage in the Halliburtons, some distance away, and was found sitting inside the screened porch in the middle of winter.

"My husband, Reg Law the lawyer, is missing."

"Who are you?"

"I am Mrs. Law."

"When did you realize he was missing?"

"I came home in the evening, around 6.30 pm from the Couchiching Peace Conference, held at the Y Geneva Park Centre out on the Rama Casino Road. I parked the car there in the driveway and noticed that my husband's car wasn't already there. So, I thought he had stepped out for a while to get a bite to eat and would soon return. I went to bed around 10.00 pm thinking he was at a meeting and would come in later. I fell sleep. In the morning, when I woke up, I noticed that his side of the bed hadn't been slept in."

"Had he ever done this before, not notified you when he was going to be absent?"

"Never. He's not like that. He's always tried to phone me or leave me a post-it sticker to let me know where he'd gone."

"When did you last see him?"

"'Yesterday. We had breakfast together, then he kissed me goodbye. He got into his car, taking his laptop and cell phone. This was around 8:30 and then I left for the all-day conference. Because the conference was nearby, I came back in the evening to sleep here instead of staying over in the lodge. Most of the conference goers stay over."

"I have to ask you this," said Clancy "was there a fight beforehand, an argument, or anything that would cause him to disappear?"

"We parted on good terms."

"Was he stressed at all? Did he have problems at work? Financial difficulties? Was he depressed?"

She gave a simple reply. "No."

"Mrs. Law, I'll file a missing persons report and keep a look out for his car. I'll need the license number. How about Constable Scott and I drop over to your place and take a look around. You may have missed something. We'll be there in about twenty minutes. The Pellatt estate properties?"

"Yes, that's right, in north Mariposa, two doors down from Judge Wiffy's home."

***

The house was large, built on three levels, brick, with a double garage for two vehicles. Rose bushes lined the cobblestone driveway leading to the large oak front door.

Clancy pressed the buzzer, setting off a ring of chimes, then glanced up at the security camera. A woman's voice on the intercom asked, "Who is it?"

"Sergeant Clancy, of the OPP."

"Hold on." He waited, then heard the sound of footsteps in the hall.

Mrs. Law looked anxious and drawn, probably hadn't gotten much sleep. She was a middle-aged woman, matronly in appearance, wearing a plain black skirt and a white shirt with a Celtic Cross pewter pin in the collar. On her feet were black ballet flats. Her hair was mouse brown, cropped to her head. A no nonsense hair style. She wore no jewelry, except her plain wedding ring and no makeup. She was dressed in a strictly casual and functional way. Not a woman to arouse strong passions in anyone.

She wasn't his cup of tea. "But one never knows", thought Clancy, "appearances are deceiving."

She sighed. "Come in and find a seat in the living room."

She led them along the silver patterned papered hall into a large room with a deep brown leather couch and big comfortable leather chairs, the kind of furniture that a big man would sit in. Opposite was a large marble fireplace above which was an empire style gold and black styled framed mirror. Too ornate for his taste. An oil painting of Queen Elizabeth sitting on a moose, painted by local artist Charles Pachter, made him smile. The artist had a great sense of humour. It hung on one wall, and a large flat TV screen, with stereo and speakers, dominated the other. "Expensive" thought Clancy. A low glass coffee table loaded with magazines: MacLean's, Canadian Lawyer, Architectural Digest, stood in front of the sofa.

Mrs. Law sat stiffly down opposite them, quickly pulling her skirt over her knees.

"We would like to ask you a few background questions. You said the last time you saw your husband was yesterday morning?"

"That's correct."

"Any reason for him to stay away all night? Do you suspect your husband of having an affair?"

"No, never. He's not like that. He's of the old school."

"And what is that?"

"Loyal and traditional. We've been married for more than twenty years. He's been faithful all those years."

"No children?"

She shook her head.

"Have you a recent photo? That will help."

She went to the desk and took an album out of the drawer. She took out a photo and handed it to him. "Here, will this do?"

It was a headshot of a man in his late forties or early fifties, His hairline had receded until there was white tufts of hair over his ears only, leaving him almost bald, but he still had black, bushy eyebrows a nice aquiline nose and large blue eyes. There was a quiet intelligence about his face.

Clancy thanked her. "We'll see what we can do. If we need to contact you during the day, where can we find you?"

"I teach English during the winter session at Georgian College, but in the summer I am at leisure. We have an answering machine if I'm out. You can leave me a message." She led them to the front door. "Please keep in touch with me until you find him," she said.

"We will, Mrs. Law. Give it a few days."

***

There had been a big storm overnight and the pavement was still damp in patches. The sewers filled with rushing water flowed into the sewer grates. The sun was on the verge of coming out from behind grey clouds.

Clancy was sitting back in his chair, slowly sipping his morning coffee while thinking about the break in and the missing lawyer, Reg Law. He was searching for his ball point pen, first in his shirt pockets, then his trousers. Empty. He drummed his fingers on the desktop. Someone had taken his pen.

Then the door flew open.

It was Mira, the man-eating journalist from the Mariposa Packet, dressed in a red V-neck cotton blouse and black miniskirt. Her face said it all.

"Whoa Mira you look a sight! What happened to your eye? Its half shut, all yellow and purple. You're limping? Back into a door?"

"Oh sure," sighed Mira, leaning on his desk with a world-weary gesture. "I am not up to scratch today. I need to sit down."

"Yeh, I can see that. Was it a rough date?"

"You can say that again."

"I have a sympathetic ear, especially for the media. You can tell me. if you want to? Pull up the chair over there and rest your feet. I won't bite."

"You haven't bitten yet. Well," said Mira, flouncing down on the chair. "it's a long story. I went up to the Roadhouse, you know, that place on the edge of town for drinks and some dancing."

"I know the place. It's where people go to get lucky. It's a regular meat market. Can't imagine you going there, you're not the type." Clancy grinned.

"Knock it off, Clancy. People meet and marry these days from people they meet in bars. It has a small band, and a lot of people go there, mostly those over twenty-five. It's good on Thursday night, if you want a date for the weekend. They have this big long bar next to the dance floor where you can comfortably sit and watch the action. There's a nice patio outside for drinking and you can order hamburgers and fries if you haven't eaten supper. I got to talking to this tall guy in leather; leather jacket, leather pants, leather stud bracelet, with lot of gold chains around his neck, wearing cowboy boots. He had a nice butt!"

"Huh? Tall dark and handsome, eh?"

"I was just doing a little market research, material for a story on bikers. You get the picture,"

"Oh please, Mira, doing market research in a bar is a bit of a stretch."

"He asked me to dance. We didn't bump into anybody. He didn't push. He was not aggressive, but polite which is nice to see in a man. He didn't give me the big feel or clamp his body to mine. He gave the attitude of 'take or leave it.' We had a few twirls on the dance floor, mostly to rock and roll and country music, then he said, it's hot in here, let's go outside. I need a cigarette.

"We walked out to the parking lot and found a secluded spot near some trees and bushes. He lit up his cigarette, smoked it halfway to the end, stubbed it out, then turned to me.

"He kissed me, a good firm kiss, which I didn't mind. Then he kissed me again using his tongue."

"I'm sure you didn't mind."

"Clancy, you're interrupting my story. He began to press himself against me, to grind his pelvis against mine. At that point I indicated that this was as far as I wanted to go. I didn't want cheap sex. I have my standards, I'll have you know. I'm not a pickup for quick sex in a parking lot. I gently pushed him away."

"Your standards are very high, Mira. I must admit."

Mira ignored Clancy's sarcasm. "He grabbed the front of my blouse and gave me a yank. He yelled, you little tease, you can't play games with me. Then he hauled off and socked me. That's how I got my black eye. I didn't expect it. He had turned on a dime into a nasty piece of work."

"Why didn't you call the police? That's physical and sexual assault. Why didn't you press charges?"

"I was in a daze. At the time, I thought about it, but then I thought was it worth the time and energy chasing after him. He had jumped on his motorcycle and left the parking lot and was just a speck in the distance by the time I recovered my senses."

"Give me a name and I'll run it through our crime data base."

"Now that you mention it, this is embarrassing to say, but I didn't get his name."

"Oh, Mira, a guy gives you a black eye, rips your blouse, and you don't know his name? You make your living as a journalist?"

"I was off duty."

"I'll say you were. Live and learn. I can't help you, Mira, but

I will keep an eye out for someone fitting that description. His motorcycle license would have helped."

"Yes, the planets are just not aligned," sighed Mira, getting up from her chair to go back to work. "Rotten luck. So much for market research. Trouble comes when you least expect it."

Clancy thought Mira should knock off the market research.

Chapter 4

Rummaging around on his desk, among the papers scattered here and there, Clancy found Reg Law's office number and address which he had gotten from Mrs. Law. Now was the time to visit the law firm, one street south of Mississauga.

He noted the black and gold lettered sign on the outside of the low-rise brick building, *Partners in Law, Law and Stone,* and went in. The reception area was large with bare brick walls. There was a small glass coffee table, with a Globe and Mail and several real estate brochures spread out on it. The receptionist sat in part of the room partitioned off with a swing gate. The sign in front of her said Lois Neat. She was a woman with intelligent eyes a and grey bangs, wearing gold knot earrings and a tiny gold cross around her neck. She must be in her late fifties thought Clancy. She had all the appearance of a legal secretary, very tidy, discreet and dependable.

He introduced himself and said. "Reg Law's wife has reported him missing. "Has he come in to work today?"

"No, he hasn't not come in and he hasn't picked up his messages or his mail."

"Can you tell me who else works here?" asked Clancy.

"It's a small partnership just two lawyers and myself. I've been with them for ten years. Reg Law does criminal defense cases and his partner, Mel Stone does real estate," answered Ms. Neat.

He wrote it down in his notebook. "What time did he leave the office?"

"At his usual time 5:30 p.m. There were no clients waiting to see him in which in case, he would have left later."

"Anything unusual happen during the day?"

"Nothing amiss. He went for a coffee break with Mel for half an hour, which seemed longer than usual."

"Do you have any idea about what they discussed?"

"He didn't say."

"When he returned, was he in a good mood? Stressed or depressed?"

"Very much the same. You will have to speak to Mr. Stone, his partner. I can't really offer you any more information. I'll buzz him and tell him you're here."

Clancy walked down the hall and knocked on the door. "Come in".

Mel Stone, an attractive male in his late forties, dressed in an expensive suit, got to his feet and they shook hands. "I wondered when you would get in touch with me."

"Why's that?"

"Reg Law, my partner, said he might contact the police about threatening phone calls. I'm glad he did."

"According to his wife, he's disappeared."

"Disappeared? Now he's missing? The conversation we had yesterday might have a bearing on his disappearance."

"Can you tell me about his background?"

"Reg Law was a long-time friend. We went to Osgoode Hall law school together. After Osgoode he articled with a large corporate law firm in downtown Toronto. After deciding that billing wealthy clients for $400.00 an hour wasn't the way he wanted to live his life, he moved to Barrie to join the Crown for about five years and then we met up and established this practice here in Mariposa."

"What did you two discuss when you talked yesterday?"

"He talked about the threatening calls he'd been receiving the last couple of months."

"Did he have any idea who called?"

"The numbers were blocked. He didn't recognize the voice. What we did do was go over who had threatened him in the past. Several criminals had threatened him when he was a crown prosecutor over in Barrie."

"Their names?"

"As I recall, if I remember correctly, Gary Falls, Joseph Bathe and Harold Steppes. They might be out now, on life-long probation. They were convicted of murder and manslaughter.

"I didn't take the threats too seriously. I figured it was some crank who had gotten hold of his phone number. I told him to go to the police and see what they could do if it keeps on. He said he didn't have much confidence in the police."

"That was your last conversation with him?"

"Yes. I'm rather worried now that something serious has happened to him. It's not like him to be gone without telling anyone. Not like him at all. Have you checked emergency at the hospital?"

"So far nothing has come in. We have the license number of his car and we will have that posted," said Clancy.

"Thanks. I'll let you know if I hear anything."

"Do that."

As Clancy walked back to the office the phone rang. It was Mrs. Law again, "Have you heard anything? Anything at all?" she asked, anxiously.

"No, nothing as yet. We're keeping our eyes and ears open."

Privately, thought Clancy, a lawyer with his kind of money has probably run off with some chick and will slink back into town when the coast has cleared.

Chapter 5

It would be nice, thought Clancy, if the day began with the sounds of birds singing, but the air was filled with the early morning sounds of the street being washed down by a water truck and the banging of garbage trucks. There was a slight humidity in the air, suggesting that it was going to be warmer later in the day. It had rained again during the night.

Clancy finished putting fresh coffee grounds into a new filter and cold water into the coffee machine. His colleagues had not come in yet.

He turned on the radio. News flash.

"Families of two fishermen who went out fishing on Lake Couchiching late last night have reported them missing. They were due to arrive home at midnight. This morning a lake search was organized. Their overturned boat has been found near the north shore with life saving jackets floating on the water beside it. Alcohol is believed to have been a factor."

This was followed by another report.

"Two missing adult male canoeists paddling up the Washago River to Washago. Their canoe tipped in waves over 2 metres high. A recovery effort is now underway."

Clancy mulled over the disappearance of Reg Law who had probably run off with a young girl leaving his boring middle-aged wife to fend for herself, the usual reason most men took off. He would turn up soon enough, sneak back into town when the coast was clear, and his wife had given up the chase.

Nevertheless, he would put out a news flash. *"Missing local lawyer, Reg Law, a middle-aged male, 6 foot, slightly bald, weight about 250 lbs. Please contact the Mariposa OPP if you have any information."*

Sitting at his desk, he slid his foot out of his shoe. His sock had a nice big hole in the toe. It was time to throw it out and buy a new pair. Agnes never darned a thing. His shirt felt tight at the waist from eating too much. He had to cut back on Agnes' generous helpings. He looked down at the back of his hand. A large red nodule that was itchy, the size of the circumference of a pencil, was growing among the black hairs, one that he hadn't noticed before. He would have to get it checked out with Dr. Sandy to make sure that it wasn't skin cancer. You can never be too careful about moles. He'd had one taken off his back, which had proved to be squamous cell carcinoma. This one might be the same, hopefully, and not melanoma.

He was interrupted in his thoughts by David dragging himself into the office. He didn't look like a happy camper. His eyes were bloodshot, and his hair needed combing.

"What's up?" asked Clancy, glancing up from his paperwork, glad for an excuse not to continue reading.

"Women are more trouble than they're worth. Nothing but trouble," said David, shaking his head. "I've got a headache."

"Have you been dipping your beak again? You're quite the dipper, David my boy. I thought you and Clara were an item and you were tied up? How wrong was I?"

"We are, we are. But she's gone off for a two-week school trip to Ottawa with her class to see the Parliament buildings, the Museum of Civilization and the eternal flame on Parliament Hill. Everything is fine. My problem was, I got a little lonely last night, so I went down for a drink at Brewery Bay." David threw up his hands. "I want to make it clear. I didn't go to pick up anybody, just to have a drink."

"Lonely boy standing at the bar. I know where this one is heading," said Clancy, smirking. David ignored his sarcasm.

"I put away a few which wasn't smart. Anyhow, to cut to the chase, sitting at the bar next to me was this chick, kind of cute, blond curls, big blue eyes, nice little breasts, a substitute teacher for Simcoe County. We talked about what we did on vacation: camping and where we'd camped. I mentioned the Bruce Trail, and Tobermory. How beautiful it was up there, especially the hiking trail on Flowerpot Island. We canoed, etc. We had a lot of similar interests. I looked at my watch. It was getting late, I told her that it was nice meeting her, but I had to go."

"She asked if I could give her a ride back to her place, a

second-floor apartment on Brant Street, not far away. She had to get up for work early too.

"I'd had about three pints and shouldn't have been driving. When we got there, she invited me in. I refused, claiming having to get up early. But then she called me chicken. So, like a dummy I went in. She had a nice little place, small but cozy, with a comfortable sofa and chairs, a TV, small kitchen and bedroom.

"She offered me black coffee, which was a good idea. We sat on her sofa and talked some more. When I finished, I put my mug down on the coffee table. The next thing I knew, she was on top of me, pulling at my leather belt. I wasn't prepared for what happened next."

Clancy gave a mock surprised smile. "My, my, life is full of surprises."

"Yeh, that's true. You won't believe me, but I didn't realize how vulnerable I was. I should have foreseen the situation before it happened. I shouldn't have taken a single woman home or gone into her place for coffee. I was just doing her a favour, trying to be a nice guy. I've learned my lesson. I'm only giving old ladies rides in my car from now on."

"Oh, tell it to the judge," said Clancy "see what he says!"

"You're so sympathetic," said David. "Anyhow things got out of control, we got carried away. We did the nasty.

"I thanked her for the coffee and told her it was a nice evening, but I had complications in my life. I didn't want her to think I was a user, a slam, bam, thank you ma'am, type of person. Or that this was a one-night stand and that I had deliberately gone to the bar to have sex, which in a way it was. She asked if I were married and I told her I was single but had a girlfriend."

"She became teary eyed. Tried to make me feel guilty for what I'd done. No, correction, for what we'd done. Asked why I hadn't told her I had a girlfriend and said things would have been different. She wouldn't have made love to me. She had feelings for me, etc.

"What a mess. What'll I do if she shows up here? She has my name and knows where I work. Dumb me."

"I'll give her the blow if she shows up here," said Clancy. "but if I know women, she won't show up here. She'll go to Brewery Bay where you met her, in the hope you'll change your mind and go there for a drink and that things will continue from where you left off.

"Oh, that I can handle. But what if Clara gets wind of this?

It could be another Hiroshima."

"What you are feeling, David, my boy, is good, old-fashioned guilt. Roll in it."

"Oh, you're a real pal, showing such sympathy, such empathy."

"My advice, and you might not take it, don't go drinking in Brewery Bay for a while. Avoid trouble before trouble finds you."

David went back to his desk and sat down. His headache was getting worse.

The phone rang. Clancy picked it up. It was the OPP dispatch office north of Mariposa.

"You're looking for a missing person, a middle-aged male. We might have something for you." The officer gave details.

After he'd hung up, Clancy called out, "David, some news. They found a body. A boy, Tim Holt, was out fishing in the lake, near the locks at Port Severn when he found the body of a middle-aged man. The only missing person we have at the moment is the lawyer, Reg Law. His wife reported him missing yesterday. It might be him."

"I can give you a little background on the area," David said. "For sailors and boaters, the headwaters at the north end of Lake Couchiching flow north into Georgian Bay, part of the Trent Canal waterway system which connects Trenton on Lake Ontario to Port Severn on Georgian Bay eastward, a distance of three hundred and eighty-seven kilometers. The system was begun in 1833 and completed in 1920.

"For boaters, there's quite a drop-in water level, over eighty metres (260) feet to reach Georgian Bay, hence the building of the locks.

"The Port Severn Lock is nineteen miles long. Known as Lock 45, it is the smallest lock on the waterway and only 1.5 metres deep. It's open 10 a.m. to 6 p.m. Monday to Friday and from 9 a.m. to 7 p.m. on the weekends.

"For boaters with boats too big for the lock, besides the lock at Port Severn is Lock 44, the Big Chute Marine Railway, the only means of transportation for getting larger boats transferred overland to the next waterway. Get this, it's the only conveyance system like that in the world, outside of Russia. By crane, the boats are hoisted onto a huge wooden platform which then conveys them on railway tracks to the next waterway, bypassing the locks to a drop of eighteen metres."

"Wow, you're an encyclopedia, David."

"Thanks to Clara, my friend, the school-teacher."

"Let's go and check this out. Divers have been called to retrieve the body. They're holding it until we get there."

They headed up north Mariposa, past the wetlands of marshes, reeds and bulrushes growing along the side of the road. A huge Osprey nest sat high on a post. "Slow down," said David, "so I can see if the osprey is on the nest."

"We may have a possible murder investigation, David. Keep focused." snapped Clancy. "Forget about birds, feathered or otherwise."

"To pass the time, I want to tell you about a suspicious death that happened there in the late 1940s. You might find it interesting. A recently married woman, Christina Kettlewell, drowned on the banks of the Severn River in a shallow pool of water, only nine inches deep. The Inquest said it was a suspicious death but didn't point to any suspects.

"No way," said David, "how could anyone drown in nine inches of water?"

"It would be difficult," said Clancy. "Well, as the story goes, the 22-year old Christina had only been married for eight days. Who did they take on their honeymoon but the best man, Ronald Barrie."

"The best man! You must be joking."

"Prior to this happy occasion, Barrie and the husband Jack Kettlewell had gone on holidays together, taking frequent trips up north which were well observed by the co-owner of the Severn Falls Marina.

"Christina and Jack had eloped because of her parents' objections to the fact that Jack wasn't Catholic. They spent the first few nights of their honeymoon in an apartment with Barrie in Toronto before heading up to the Port Severn cottage owned by Barrie, bringing Barrie with them."

"How odd can you get?"

"A fire broke out at the cottage, burning it to the ground. The two men escaped. Christina's body, clad in pajamas, was found on the riverbank face down in a shallow pool of river water, with no burn marks or sign of violence on her body. The only thing found in her stomach by the coroner was codeine.

"At the inquest, Barrie, formerly known as Ronnie Ciufo, produced two letters saved from the burned cottage to provide grounds for Christina's suicide. In one she wrote … "and if I can't have him, I don't intend anyone else to… I now realize I am just a passing fancy."

"How convenient," said David, "to be able to save these letters from a cottage that burned to the ground. It's strange that they were addressed to Barrie and not her husband. Stranger too, that he didn't warn her husband about her suicidal nature."

"Handwriting experiments testified that it was her writing." said Clancy," but there's more, Barrie was named as the beneficiary on two separate $5,000 life insurance policies that Jack and Christina had taken out before they eloped. The policies carried a double indemnity provision, meaning two times the amount would be paid out to Barrie in the case of accidental death."

"Why did Jack cut his family out of his will, hand earnings to Barrie and let his friend tag along on his honeymoon?" asked David

"Jack admitted in a statement entered in court to a long-term love affair with Barrie. But, when faced with the document and his signature, Jack testified that it was police entrapment that made him sign it.

"At the inquest because of the suspicious fact that Christina was found drowned in nine inches of water, the jury delivered an open verdict in the case, unable to agree on whether foul play was involved.

"Get this. Jack wasn't gay. Jack remarried three years later and had a family. Sometime later Barrie disappeared to live in New York, and nothing was heard or seen of him again.

"Interesting little story, huh? That Barrie guy sounded like a real piece of work. Poor Christina for getting mixed up with them," said David.

"It wouldn't go down that like that today. There would be all kinds of toxicology tests, and the insurance companies wouldn't pay out like they did at that time," said Clancy.

It took them about half an hour driving up Highway 17 to get there past rolling countryside. In some fields there were cows grazing. In another, horses, sheep and goats were nibbling. A few chickens were wandering in the ditch at the side of the road.

"It's hard to imagine," said David, "that this land used to be covered by glaciers. When the Ice Age ended and the ice melted, it left behind pockets of hills and valleys. That's why it's called rolling countryside, a terrain of fields and hills."

"That school-teacher of yours is really enlarging your brain," said Clancy.

When they got to the lake, the corpse had been fished out of the water and was lying on a black plastic tarp. Looking closer, they could see that the body was covered in green algae, with brackish water leaking from the nose, and ears. A large, black beetle crawled out of its mouth. The eyes bulged and the tongue stuck out. Black flies were circling over the body. Clancy gagged at the smell and sight of this middle-aged man lying shoeless before them

The coroner's car was already parked by the side of the road and Dr. Frost was looking over the dead body.

Clancy looked closer. It could be Reg Law. "Any idea of time of death?"

"Approximately two days ago, but that is all I can tell you at this point. The body has not been in the water long, no serious decomposition. There is a nasty contusion on the back of his head. See here, where the hair is parted. The blood has been washed away," said Dr. Frost.

"Did he hit his head on something or was he whacked and then dumped into the lake?" asked Clancy. Thankfully, the locks were closed, so the body could be found here, otherwise it would have been taken by water currents all the way to Georgian Bay by now. "Does it look like murder?" asked Clancy.

"An autopsy will tell us more," said Dr. Frost," don't jump to any conclusions, but the back of his head looks pretty bashed in for it to be called an accident caused by the body falling into the lake.".

"If it is murder, and it looks like it, the murderer is pretty clever, the water would wash away all that DNA evidence," said Clancy.

Dr. Frost nodded. He stood up to indicate he was finished and waved for the police to zip the body into the black plastic body bag which would be taken in a hearse down to Mariposa for the autopsy.

Chapter 6

      Now to notify the next of kin and get a positive identification down at the morgue thought Clancy, a prospect that he was not looking forward to. This was one of the most difficult parts of his job. Although there was no cell phone or ID on the dead body, there was a strong chance that it was Reg Law, but someone would have to formally identify him. That would be his wife.
      The sun was high in the sky. It was going to be another hot day. Clancy turned on the car's air conditioner. Both he and David were silent, each with his own thoughts as they drove back to north Mariposa to the large 3-storey red house with the rose bush borders. The blinds had been drawn and the house looked deserted. After parking the car, Clancy buzzed and waited. The intercom came on and he identified himself and his partner.
      Mrs. Law answered the door and led them wordlessly into the living room, indicating for them to sit down. She had no make-up on and this time was dressed in sport slacks and a white sport shirt.
      "We prefer to stand," said Clancy. "We've come with some bad news, Mrs. Law. They've located the body of a middle-aged man in the lake near the locks up at Port Severn. Are you acquainted with that area?"
      "Of course," said Mrs. Law. "It's very familiar to Reg and me. We would go up there to the Riverhouse Restaurant, which has a lovely outdoor patio, for good homemade food. We'd often go up there for dinner and sit outdoors and watch the boats come in. It has a nice marina. It was very relaxing to sit there in the evening."
      "Well that was where the body was found."

"Oh no," said Mrs. Law," sitting down. "I hope that it's not Reg. What would he be doing up there so far, from Mariposa, without me?"

"We need you to identify the body. Will you gather your things and come with us? We're going to the morgue in the basement of Soldiers Memorial Hospital."

"I'll be just a minute. Wait while I get my purse."

Mrs. Law got into the back seat of the car showing little emotion, but her hands were tightly gripping her black leather purse. A cool one, thought Clancy

They drove into the parking lot and went through the front door, heading for the basement which was cool any time of the year. Clancy always found the walk to the morgue depressing, with its grey tiles and darkened corridor. The attendant, Mel Hat, in green scrubs gave them a quick glance as they passed and a little wave of recognition.

Through the intercom in the viewing room, Clancy identified himself, then called for the body found that morning to be brought out. Silently they stood waiting.

Clancy held Mrs. Law's elbow to steady her as the minutes slowly ticked by. Then, the white curtain was pulled back and they could see through the window.

The body of Reg Law lay before them, with a white sheet covering him up to his chin.

Mrs. Law took a deep breath, then tears began falling down her cheeks splashing onto the front of her shirt.

She finally said, "Yes, that's my husband, Reg Law. How could this happen?"

"We don't know, Mrs. Law," said Clancy, leading her away from the window, "but we'll find the person who did this. Did he have any enemies that you know of? Did he mention anyone who was bothering him?"

"None that I know of."

"A female constable will drive you back to your residence. I imagine you will want to rest after this."

"Yes, it's quite a shock coming out of the blue with no warning, with no sign of anything."

"After an autopsy to determine cause of death, the body will be released to you as the next of kin. It will take maybe two weeks at the most."

"I plan to have my husband's body cremated and then have a memorial service at the church later in the fall. I will contact Mr.

Miller, the funeral director, to make the arrangements. I don't have the emotional energy to hold a public funeral at the moment, with this hanging over me."

"I understand. Thank you for your co- operation, Mrs. Law."

Chapter 7

Back at the office, Clancy said to David. "I want to speak to Tim Holt to see what he has to tell us. We were so busy with the body that I didn't get a chance to speak to him. Maybe he can give us more details. It's worth a try."

Clancy drove up the Port Severn Road to try to find Tim Holt at the address that he had given him. He knocked on the wooden front door of his home, a modest, one-storey brick house on a side road, with a truck in the driveway and several old dilapidated cars marooned on the front lawn.

His mother, in an apron and slacks, came to the door.

"I'm here to speak to Tim. I'm just making inquiries," said Clancy. "I need his help."

"Oh yes, is it about that awful drowning at the locks yesterday? He's not here. He's gone fishing over at the park near the locks. That's where he usually fishes."

Clancy got back into his car and drove over. He easily found the lone figure of the preadolescent youth standing with his rod at the edge of the small lake.

"Hey, Tim, "Clancy called out and then flashed his ID. "Good to see you again. How often do you come here?"

"A couple of times a week, usually after school. But now that school is out, I come every day."

"What's the fishing like?"

"Not bad, I usually catch a trout or a perch."

"Good place to fish?"

"Yeh, lots of little marine plants for the fish to feed on."

"Did you see anything the day before you found the body in

the water? Or that evening? Was there anything different or unusual that you can remember?"

"No."

"Was there anyone around but yourself?"

"I was just here by myself."

"Did you notice anything strange or odd?"

"No."

"Well, thanks Tim, for your help. I'll leave you my card, call me if you think of anything."

***

While he was in the area Clancy decided he might as well check out the Riverhouse Restaurant. Mrs. Law had mentioned that she and her husband had often dined there. Maybe Reg Law had gone there that evening before he was murdered. Clancy wanted to trace his movements before he was murdered. Better talk to the staff.

He drove up to the restaurant. He pushed the door open, walked past the bar seating area, and found a young waitress, probably summer help, at the back folding a pile of paper napkins.

She looked up and smiled. "We won't be open for supper until five o'clock, but you can order bar food and beer on the patio at the back."

"No, I'm not here to dine, Miss." He showed her his ID. "I want to ask you about someone who came here sometimes for dinner. His name is Reg Law. Here's his picture."

She studied it for a few minutes. "He looks familiar."

"When was he last here?"

'Two nights ago, around half five, I think."

"Was he alone?"

"No, he was with a young woman."

"Do you know who she was?"

"No idea."

"Did he bring her here more than once?"

"Several times. I don't think she was his wife. I've seen him here with an older, plain woman several times. This one was rather pretty and young."

Clancy put the photo away. "Thanks for your help. If you think of anything else, here's my card."

Well that puts a different spin on things. Who was the young woman in question and where can I find her, thought Clancy

Chapter 8

Clancy drove down the highway slowing down at the Osprey's nest to see whether the bird was sitting on it. The nest was empty, but a lovely fawn was standing by the roadside nibbling on blueberries. He slowed down so as not to startle the young animal.

Back in the office, he related to David what the waitress had told him.

David was not surprised. "The old boys get up to it every time, especially the restless middle- aged ones." The phone rang.

"It's for you, Clancy. It's Agnes." Clancy mumbled a few words under his breath.

"Don't forget to stop and pick up the pork chops at No Frills. We can have a barbecue tonight if the weather remains good."

"Will do," said Clancy, writing it down. Agnes always had something for him to bring home for dinner.

The phone rang again. "Dr. Frost speaking. Reg Law's autopsy is scheduled for ten tomorrow, if you're interested. Be on time."

"Thanks," said Clancy, thinking he should have a light breakfast before going, just coffee and toast.

**

Today his shift was over, time to head out. Back at home, Clancy fired up the barbecue. For dinner they were having pork chops which he'd bought. Agnes had made a nice garden salad to go with it.

He sat down on the lawn chair and took a sip of cold beer. It was nice to sit out in the backyard with the fresh breeze blowing up from the lake, doing nothing but navel gazing.

Chapter 9

Promptly at 10 a.m., Clancy drove over to the parking lot at Soldiers Memorial Hospital. The hospital charged a lot for public parking and there was no way he could park for free, only 'In Emergency'. This wasn't an emergency. Where to park? In a doctor's space for a short time, he decided.

He walked down the steps into the basement where the autopsy would be held. Dr. Frost in hairnet, goggles, and slippers was waiting for him. He greeted Clancy briskly, "You're on time. Good."

They waited while Mel Hat rolled the body onto a gurney from the refrigerated shelf then brought it over to the stainless-steel table. It took a few minutes to get everything in place and the high overhead lights switched on.

The body of Reg Law was laid out as cold as marble on the stainless-steel table. Clancy's mask filtered out the smell.

After noting height and weight, Dr. Frost began his examinations beginning with the head. "There's a large contusion on the back of the head. Here, feel it. Someone may have hit him there with a blunt instrument, or he fell and hit his head, on something in the water. But I don't think so. Look at the arms." H e held up one and then the other. "There are nail scratches, and knife cuts on the skin. Defense wounds."

After he had examined the exterior of the body, Dr. Frost made a Y cut into the torso, then the cut through the rib cage to get at the heart, the lungs and other internal organs.

"He was alive when he was pushed into the water. That's what the air in his lungs tell us. Then he drowned."

Dr. Frost peeled away the scalp, down to the eyes. "There it is, the hematoma, the blood swelling on the brain. We will have that sliced and put on sections of glass."

"So did the injury occur before he hit the water?" asked Clancy.

"The contusion is too big and deep, just to be obtained by entering the water. I think it was an unnatural death, caused by blunt trauma, done by persons unknown."

Chapter 10

Who did it? Back at the office, the first alibi to check out was Mrs. Law. Her motive would be anger and jealousy, if she'd found out about her husband's relationship with another woman. Clancy phoned the conference centre of the Geneva Park YMCA and spoke to the receptionist. "Do you have a list of attendees at the Couchiching Peace Conference held a few days ago? I'm looking for a name, that of Mrs. Reg Law."

"Give me a minute and I'll see what I can do. The list should be around somewhere. Got it. Mrs. Law? According to our records, she paid for the day conference but didn't stay overnight in the lodge."

"How long did the conference last?"

"It started at nine, then a coffee break at ten, then lunch at one and carried on until eight pm."

"Did you notice whether anyone left early?"

"I'll ask Mr. Jameson. He works on the desk. He attended. Just a minute please."

"No. Everyone stayed right to the end," said Mr. Jamieson.

Clancy thanked him. That left a window of a couple of hours for which Mrs. Law had no alibi. The problem with her being the murderer was, would she have the strength to drag her husband's body and dump him in the lake? Clancy hardly thought so. He was a big man and weighed more than she did. Impossible, unless Mrs. Law had an accomplice. Well it's a beginning.

The other question was, where was Reg Law's car? How did he get up to the restaurant? He came in a car with a young woman who had vanished. "David," said Clancy, "put out a bulletin with the license plate number and we'll see if someone comes across it."

***

The next task was to get busy investigating who had been threatening Reg Law. He had been given three names by Mel Stone, these needed to be checked out. The first name on the list was Gary Falls.

The last address that the parole board had was in Barrie. He might be living there or have moved on. Clancy decided on taking a chance on that address

It was a nice drive down Highway 11, from Mariposa to Barrie, not as crowded as Highway 400, just a pleasant half hour with little traffic through the farmland of Medonte County, passing a few country churches, Shaw's Sugar Bush Farm ,a store that sold farm equipment, another which sold trailer homes.

When he arrived at Barrie's harbour, he drove along to an apartment building and rang the buzzer for Gary Falls. No answer. Again, he rang it. On the third ring, an overweight man with a cane shuffled to the door. "I'm slow answering the door, because I've got arthritis in my feet real bad."

"I'm trying to locate Gary Falls. Are you Gary?"

"Yeh. How can I help you?"

"Just a few questions. I won't take up much of your time." Clancy identified himself. "Can I come in?"

"Yes, that would be okay. Normally I don't let strangers in. My wife has gone out to do some shopping."

"I didn't know that you had remarried."

"About five years ago. When I was in Kingston Pen my sister knew this nice woman who was lonely and lived here in Barrie. She told her about me. She wrote to me and I wrote back. We corresponded. She came and visited me in the Pen. I told her what I was in for. I held nothing back. Anyhow, when I got out we got married. My two kids from my first marriage have scattered like the wind, gone their own separate ways, doing their own thing. We were never close. So here at the house there's just the two of us. I'm living on my old age pension and social security."

Gary took him into a living room. A German Shepherd jumped up onto the sofa, preparing to sit down. "Get down, boy," shouted Falls.

"I've come to ask you if you knew Reg Law." Clancy produced a picture.

He shook his head. "The name is not familiar."

"This goes back a long way. He's the Crown who prosecuted you in the Niagara Falls murder case."

"Oh, him." Gary looked down at his feet. "I wondered when you were going to bring that up."

"Yeh, him. You threatened that you would get him when you got out of prison. He was found murdered, drowned near the locks at Port Severn. I'm making inquiries. Where were you three nights ago?"

"Home here with the missus. She will vouch for me. Do you want to wait here until she gets back? She'll tell you."

"No, I don't have time. I'll contact you again by phone." Clancy got up to go, but he'd already reached a conclusion. This guy, Falls, is lame, arthritic, and in his senior years. I don't think he'd have had the strength or the ability to kill Reg Law and drag his body into the lake. One down, two more to go.

Chapter 11

In his pursuit of suspects, Clancy decided to strike while the iron was hot. The next name on the list was Joseph Bathe, another of the names Mel Stone gave him who had been threatening Reg. Law. He had been in Warkworth, a medium security prison, doing about fifteen years for second degree murder. It was possible that he was now out on parole with time off for good behavior. He'd look his name up in the parole system and then go an interview him.

Clancy found an address and a phone number. Joseph Bathe had returned to his hometown of Barrie after he had completed his sentence. Clancy gave him a ring. On the first couple of tries, Bathe didn't answer, only hearing a recording message, Clancy left his number. Finally, late in the day, around suppertime, Clancy called and said he would like to have a chat with him.

"What's this about? I've done my time and don't want to be harassed."

"I just want to ask you a few questions," said Clancy. "I'll be over in half an hour."

On the highway into Barrie, near the A & W, Tim Hortons, Wendy's and Burger King, he found the small one-storey house. The front lawn was covered in weeds and debris. A pink plastic flamingo stood in the centre of the yard with a paint chipped gnome off to one side. Tacky, thought Clancy, very tacky. The eavestrough was hanging from the roof with no visible means of support. An old Chevy was parked in the driveway. Clancy went up to the front door and knocked. On the third knock, the man whom he assumed was Joseph Bathe came to the door. He was a tall man, slightly stooped with a shock of grey hair.

"Joseph Bathe?" asked Clancy identifying himself.

In a gravelly voice the man answered, "First and last time I am going to answer any questions you've got. I've done my time, paid for my crime and I owe nobody anything."

"Can I come in?"

"Only if it's short and sweet."

Inside, Clancy looked around at the cluttered room, at the sagging sofa with the springs hanging out, the stacks of old newspapers piled high in the corner, and plastic bags full of garbage waiting to be taken out. A kettle and a dirty teacup stood on a draining board.

He must live alone, thought Clancy. Who would want to spend time with him in this dump?

"Do you recognize the name, Reg Law? Does that name ring a bell?" Clancy showed him the photo.

"Can't say I do."

"Let me help you. He was the Crown who put you away. You threatened him after being sentenced. You said that when you got out you would get him."

"Did I? Well that was a long time ago. I've said many things since then."

"Yes, well he was found murdered, in the lake with a nasty bump on the back of his head."

"Do you think an old guy like me is chasing after old scores or is even interested? Time has passed. I have to get on with my life."

"Where were you three nights ago?"

"Watching TV. What else is there to do?"

"Somebody watched it with you?"

"No. just me."

"How do you spend your days?"

"Collecting pogey. Wandering around. No one wants to hire an old ex con."

"Do you go wandering up around Port Severn?"

"Wherever."

"That's where the murder took place."

"Is that so. Well I wasn't there. I was here in Barrie, watching TV. I've done my time. Stop bothering me."

Clancy closed his notebook. Not a good murder suspect, judging by his physical appearance, but you can't always tell a book by its cover.

Chapter 12

Clancy drove back to the office. Greg was sitting at his desk and a little old lady was standing in front of him, holding a frail hand to her chest. He recognized her, Miss Temple.

"What can I do for you, Madam?" asked Greg.

"I need a glass of water. My heart is fluttering."

"Right. I'll get you one. Sit down." He pulled up a chair close to his desk. "Are you suffering a heart attack? Do you need an ambulance?"

"No, no, if I could just sit down and rest for a few minutes then I'll be okay and on my way."

She sat down in a chair that he brought over and slowly sipped the water. Greg thought, there's nothing like having cardiac arrest in a police station.

"Is there anything I can get you? Anyone that you'd want me to call?"

"No, I'll be fine. It's happened before." The old lady looked over at Clancy who had buried his head in paperwork on his desk, "How is your day going?"

"Fine, so far," muttered Clancy. "It could get worse."

"Yes, you must have a lot on your mind with this murder to solve and that big robbery at Judge Wiffy's. Have you gotten any clues yet?"

"Madam," said Clancy raising his voice just a little, "silence is golden."

"Ah," she said, "you want to keep it to yourself. I understand. I would too if I were in your position. You're in a very sensitive job." She drained the rest of her glass. "You've been most kind." She got up to go. "If I see or hear anything, you people will be the first to know."

"I'm sure we will," muttered Clancy under his breath.

***

"There's a news bulletin out of Barrie." said David, coming over to Clancy's desk. "Here's the printout for you."

'Down by the harbour, a jogger out for his morning run came around a corner and collided with a senior out for a walk. The senior was knocked to the ground and suffered a cardiac arrest. The victim was known to police as Terry Falls who, years ago, had been convicted of pushing his wife over the gorge at Niagara Falls. After serving time in prison he had been released on a lifetime parole and had since remarried. He leaves behind a widow and two adult children.'

"That's him," said Clancy. "That's the guy I went to interview the other day. Well that eliminates one suspect."

***

"The phone rang. "For you, Clancy." said Greg cheerfully. He knew bad news was at the other end. He recognized the voice of Clancy's wife.

"Hello," said Clancy. "Oh, it's you, Agnes. What is it? We're pretty busy here at the moment. There's a lot of heavy-duty thinking going on."

"The wasps which bothered us the other night when we were eating outdoors on the patio? A swarm of them is trying to build a nest under the eaves of the garage. I want you to get rid of them tonight when you get home. Be prepared."

"What? How do I get rid of wasps?"

"Use a taper, light it and smoke them out. Set fire to their nest if necessary, without burning down the garage."

Oh, migawd, thought Clancy and get stung in the process. He'd need long sleeves, his pant cuffs tied close to his legs, gloves and a hat pulled down around his ears. Agnes wanted him to do something dangerous.

When he drove into the driveway, he could see Agnes. like a sergeant major, standing at the living room window, pointing to the wasp nest at the side of the garage. He carefully got out, took out a newspaper that he'd picked up at the office, rolled it up, then lit the end of the paper taper with his lighter and held it up to the eaves trough where the wasps were buzzing in circles. He let the black smoke engulf the nest. Startled, most of the wasps flew up and away with a loud buzz. But one or two lingered behind and angrily flew towards him.

He felt the first sting on his ankle. The second on his wrist, which he swatted at but missed, and then the third was on his behind, bitten right through his trousers. Nasty beasts. Was he allergic to wasps? He would soon find out. Did they leave their stinger in the wound? If they did, it would have to be pulled out. Another sting. He was in pain.

"Get some baking soda quick, Agnes. They got me."

"Oh, you poor baby, lie down and I'll get your favourite drink while I pull out the stingers with my eyebrow tweezers".

"Oh, I should have paid a professional to come and do that."

"Yes, that's true but you don't like to part with the money. Calm yourself and sip your drink. The stinging won't last long"

Clancy lay back in a cloud of pain and thought about how foolish he could get.

Chapter 13

Clancy glanced over at David. "We've got to find Reg Law's missing car. When we do that it'll give us some clues. We also have to find and interview his girlfriend. She seems to have disappeared.

"After our coffee, we should go out and scout around. First place to look would be near where the body was found. How about we take a spin, a nice break from here, and drive around Port Severn locks to see if the car has been left by the road-side or parked illegally in the area."

They drove up Highway 11, past rolling countryside, fields of green and yellow. There was very little traffic on the two-lane road going north, just the odd pothole.

Suddenly, out of the bushes bounded a small black bear heading straight for their car.

Clancy pressed hard on the brakes. "Don't want to make roadkill out of him. His mother may be nearby, and she could get real nasty if we come between her and her cub. This is berry season. They're hunting for the berries. Don't go pissing in the bushes, David, or you'll be chow for a bear."

"I'll remember that."

The radio crackled. *Amber alert for a young boy, eight years old, with brown hair and brown eyes. Abducted by his father after a parental visit. Believed to be travelling in a red Ford. Believed to be heading for US Border.*

"Not in this neck of the woods," replied David.

A farmer on a tractor, hauling a huge combine, came out of a lane in front of them, travelling as slow as molasses. Clancy had to slow to a crawl behind him. "Couldn't he have waited until we were past?"

Then a senior, acting as if he were out for a Sunday afternoon drive, pulled out in front of them at the next intersection, doing way less than the speed limit. Clancy, who had no patience at all, shook his fist at him.

Finally, they were able to pass him. The rest of the stretch up to Port Severn was quiet. They arrived at the parkland of grass and trees which surrounded the blue painted locks, then began checking license plates of vehicles parked nearby. It was slow work, hot and muggy, and Clancy could feel his shirt damp under his armpits.

"If the car is parked up here, shouldn't we check the parking lot overlooking the lake? He may have driven up there for the view after dining at the Riverhouse Restaurant. If they were making out, he'd want to do it in an isolated spot," suggested David.

"Good thinking," said Clancy.

At the far end of the parking lot, there was one car that stood out, a black Chev. "This might be it," said David. When they got closer, they could see that the driver's window had been smashed in. David tried the door. It was unlocked. He looked in the glove compartment for identification records. Registration papers said the vehicle's owner was Reg Law. He figured as much. He searched the car, but it was empty of anything, clothing, cell phone, laptop, nothing tied to the owner.

"Pop the trunk," ordered Clancy.

David went to the rear of the car. An awful smell was coming out of it, a smell of decay, sweetness, rotting flesh. The hairs on his neck stood on end.

He popped the trunk. Inside, they saw the outline of a body wrapped loosely in a soggy, bloody car blanket. The smell was overpowering. When they pulled the blanket away, he saw it was the body of a young woman. Her wrists and ankles were tightly bound with rope. Her face and shoulders were a green hue. Her eyes bulged and her tongue protruded from her mouth. She was very dead.

David went to the side of the car and gagged.

"Send for forensics and scene of the crime officers," said Clancy. "Take lots of picture and contact the coroner." He lifted the blanket again to have a second look. "I don't recognize her, do you, David? She might be the young woman who dined with Reg Law at the restaurant that night. Could be anybody. We'll get a photo taken to see if anyone can identify her. Is there a purse or wallet in the trunk? No? What about Reg Law's cell phone, his laptop? Do you see them? No? O.K. They're missing."

They waited for about twenty minutes for Dr. Frost to arrive and directed him to the body lying in the trunk.

"It was good that you caught me in time, because I was just about to start on another autopsy. What have we got here?"

"A young woman."

Dr. Frost got out his rubber gloves and put them on. He lifted the lolling head slowly turning it from side to side, noticing the bruises on each side of the face.

"How long has she been dead, Doc?"

"I would say approximately three or four days. I can't say more. Rigor mortis has come and gone. Not much decomposition."

"Would you say that the time of death was somewhere in the same period when Reg Law died?" asked Clancy.

"That will be determined later."

"After you're through, we'll have the car wrapped and taken down on a lorry to the Forensic Science lab in Toronto and have them do a thorough going over to pick up fibers and fingerprints."

Chapter 14

"We need to find out who she is and tell her next of kin," said Clancy, "but first we need a name and an address. There's no phone or purse in the trunk. What is complicating this situation is that no young woman has been reported missing, which would have helped. We should drop in on our way back to the office and see Mrs. Law again and show her the photo of the woman and see if she can identify her. Also, I want to see her reaction to the fact that her husband was out with another woman. Was she aware that her husband was running around?"

When they came back though North Mariposa, they entered again the low-lying marshland. High on a wooden platform with lots of twigs and leaves was the large osprey's nest. A large, bored looking, osprey, with its massive wings spread out was standing on the edge of the platform looking down at them.

"Hey, look at that," said David, "Isn't that impressive?"

"Keep your mind on what we have to do to solve the murder," ordered Clancy," that bird can look after herself."

They found the Law house with the living room blinds closed. It looked deserted. A gardener was sitting atop a noisy lawn mower cutting the grass. He waved at them as they approached. "Nice day, eh?"

At the front door, they buzzed and waited. They rang again. Finally, a voice on the intercom asked, "Who's there?"

"OPP."

They heard the sound of footsteps echoing on the hall floor. Then the door slowly opened.

"Mrs. Law, can you help us. We've found your husband's car.

It will be returned to you after forensics down in Toronto is through with it, perhaps in two weeks. A young woman was found dead in the trunk. We want to see if you can identify the photo of her."

"Oh no, how can that be?" Mrs. Law's face turned pale.

"Here's the photo." Clancy showed her his cell phone. He watched the expressions on her face, her eyes particularly, as she was handed the picture.

"Have you seen that young woman before?"

Mrs. Law was adamant, "No, most certainly not."

"Are you sure?" He watched for a change of expression on her face.

"No, I'm sorry," Mrs. Law was indignant, "I fail to recognize her. What was her body doing in the trunk of my husband's car? I've never seen her before. I have no idea who she is."

"That's what we want to find out. Someone placed her in your murdered husband's trunk after killing her. We have to find out how the two were connected. Do you think that your husband might have been having an affair with that young woman?"

She said stiffly. "My husband was very faithful. He wouldn't contemplate doing such a thing. It would be completely out of character."

Clancy let his silence speak for what he thought. Of course, he was having an affair with that young woman. "Well, Mrs. Law, that's all our questions at the moment. We will keep in touch."

Chapter 15

They drove back to the office. On a hunch Clancy decided to contact Reg Law's office, the murdered woman might have some connection with it. She may have worked there and that's how Reg Law met her. Lois Neat, the office secretary, was busy on the phone. When she finished, she turned to them and asked, "what can I do for you?"

"I have a photo of a young female and want to know if you recognize her."

He held the photo in front of her- the face of a young woman with tight brown curls circling her head, a little snub nose, and large full lips. Each ear lobe held a tiny gold cross earring. Dr. Frost had closed her eyes and her mouth.

Lois Neat looked at the photo a long time before she said anything.

"It could be. I'm not certain. It has been a few months since we hired her. She used to work in this office as a temporary typist, typing up legal documents for Reg. We hired her on a part time basis whenever there was a work overload. It's Debbie Love. Why do you want to know? Has she done anything? Why? What has happened to her?"

"She's been found murdered in the trunk of Reg Law's car."

Miss Neat gasped. "Debbie Love? Murdered? In the truck of Reg Law's car? Unbelievable."

"Did you know if they were going out, or having some sort of relationship?"

"Not that I know of. It would be news to me. She came to work and left."

"Was she overly friendly with Mr. Law? Did she flirt with him or anything like that? Did she hang around the office after work? Did he offer to give her a lift home?"

"No to all your questions. You will have to ask Mel Stone, his partner. If there was a relationship, he would know."

She picked up the phone and called him. "Clancy Murphy of the OPP is here to see you about a missing girl."

'You may go right in." She gestured to a door down the hall. Clancy walked down the hall lined with law diplomas and several other group pictures of sports teams.

"What brings you here?" asked Mel Stone.

"A missing girl."

"A missing girl?" he asked, clearing away some papers from his desk. "Dreadful news about Reg. But I've already given you some names, people that he said he thought threatened him. Has anything come of that?"

"No, I'm afraid it's more bad news. We finally found his car. There was a young woman found dead, bound hand and foot in the trunk. We're trying to establish a connection. I have a photo of her and would like to hear what you have to say. Apparently, she worked here as a temp. According to your secretary, Miss Neat, her name was Debbie Love."

Mel took the photo and looked at it. "Yes, I believe that's her. I'm not a hundred per cent certain. Not a good picture, though. She worked here off and on."

"We're trying to establish what connection she had with Reg Law. Did she go out with Law at all? Was there something going on between them?"

"There may have been. I'm not discounting that. Off hand I don't know. He must have been very discreet about it. I never saw them together."

"Did Law say anything to you about her, or the fact that he was seeing her?"

"Nothing at all. He kept it secret from me. Besides this is a small town, word could easily get around. He had a wife to think of. Do the police think he murdered her, then killed himself?"

"It's a theory but it's early stages yet. Did you know much about her? Where she went in her time off?"

"She went for the odd drink after work down at Brewery Bay on Mississauga. But that's all I know. Ask around."

"If you hear anymore, let us know." Clancy handed Stone his card and made his way out.

Chapter 16

The next day was another warm one with high humidity. Clancy raised his eyes from the paperwork on his desk and spied a black cockroach heading towards a doughnut crumb on the floor. He lifted his foot and quickly smashed it. "We'd got to keep this place clean or we'll have a big roach problem and then have to bring in Pest Control." This he said to no one in particular. Greg was out on calls. David was busy at his desk, and Clancy wondered who would drop in. He didn't have to wonder long. The door blew open.

Mira, in a black leather miniskirt, red wedge heels, and a blouse that seemed to bounce up and down with every step she took, sailed into the office and smacked her notebook and pen down on his desk in front of him.

"You're brown as a berry, Mira."

"Tasty, too. I might add."

"I notice, Mira, that there's a brace on your knee. What happened to you? Did you knee anyone in the groin?"

"Funny, ha, ha." Mira glared at him. "I was hiking last weekend on Tobermory's Flowerpot Island, on the Lighthouse Trail going to the top of the island, when I twisted my knee. I hit a rock. It was very painful. I was lucky to be able to hobble back to the boat."

"My, Mira, I never thought you were an outdoor type. More indoors. definitely indoors."

"I have talents in both areas," said Mira smugly.

"I'm sure you have."

"What have you got for me, today? Greg has been most helpful in the past. You're not so helpful." said Mira.

"I'm sure he has. Mira, I need a favour from you."

"How will you repay the favour? Don't think that one drink

"Leave that up to me. I want **a** photo of the woman, Debbie Love, who was found murdered, bound and gagged in the trunk of Greg Law's car, to be blown up to see if anyone recognizes. Here's the scoop. The body of missing lawyer, Reg Law was found by a boy out fishing near Severn Lock 45. Then we went looking for his car and we finally found it not far away. In the trunk, we found a woman's body**.** Dr. Frost says she's only been dead a couple of days. We are trying to get the best reading on the time of death. So, we have two murders to solve and we need your help."

"I'm glad to see that the ball is in my court for a change. Or should I say balls? Do you think the woman was Reg Law's girlfriend?"

"We don't know. The wife denies any funny business was going on. She says she doesn't recognize her. But time will tell."

"That's what the wives always say. Do you think he killed her and then committed suicide?"

"That is a possibility, but rather far fetched. Dr. Frost has a thumb print found on her throat and will confirm or deny that it was Reg Law's.

"What we want from you and your paper is to ask your readers if anyone saw anything several days ago out at the headland near the locks. Somebody must have seen something. A car parked there, a man lingering around there, anything."

"Sounds interesting. I'm sure my paper will be happy to oblige."

"Oh, Mira, look after your knees and practice holding a quarter between them."

"Really witty, Clancy. I will collect on this favour. Don't you forget it," said Mira as she sailed out of the door.

Chapter 17

Clancy shoved aside some papers from head office marked 'Urgent.' Someone, probably Detective Bob White, at OPP Headquarters with sticky fingers wanted another statistics report which he didn't have time for. Statistics. statistics and more statistics.

Thank gawd his kids were away at camp for a little archery, swimming, and marshmallow roasting. At home, after school had ended, everything he had suggested for them to do had been too boring. He didn't want confrontation and the look on their faces staring at him over the breakfast table after they had asked what there was to do drove him nuts. Plenty, he'd replied, but everything he'd suggested had met with resistance.

Jack, his dog, also wanted attention and, when he wasn't getting it, he would go to the pile of shoes left by the front door, pick one up, shake it and dance around the living room with it in his mouth. But Jack was in his bad books. He'd eaten the heel of a bedroom slipper and now Clancy had to buy a new pair.

The silence in the office was heavenly. No wife, no kids.

Today was his appointment with Dr. Sandy to see about the reddish, purple nodule on the back of his hand.

He drove over to Soldiers Memorial and parked in a parking lot next to it, the Medical Arts building where Dr. Sandy had his office. He was buzzed in. Along the hall he could see the office door open and a sign saying, *'Don't block the hallway with baby carriages.'* He squeezed into a seat in a crowded waiting room full of people with coughs, sniffles and red eyes. One woman had her arm in a sling. She had fallen off a ladder when cleaning out the eaves-troughs on her roof she told him. A little boy was whimpering because he had been stung by a wasp.

The medical secretary finally called out Clancy's name. He got up and went in. Dr. Sandy, in his white coat and with a stethoscope greeted him, taking off his horn-rimmed glasses, polishing them with a handkerchief and then putting them back on.

"What brings you here?"

Clancy extended the back of his hand. The red nodule was changing colour and now had a purple edge.

"Don't get anxious until we have the lab report back. I'll just anaesthetize the skin and do a little biopsy. It might be nothing at all," said Dr. Sandy. "I'll have the results back in a few days. I'll call you." After the procedure, he slapped a band aid on it.

Clancy thanked him and went back to his office. He settled into his chair to mull things over. "I spy with my little eye some loose change on the floor, a loonie and a toonie. Have you got a hole in your pocket, Greg?" asked Clancy.

Greg stood up and felt in his pockets, then shook his head.

Clancy grinned. "No? Well, it's finders keepers, losers weepers." Clancy made a dive for the change and put it in his pocket.

"It probably fell out of the coffee tin. That means no coffee," said Greg with an 'I told you so' look.

"By the way how was the robbery investigation at Judge Wiffy's going?"

"Haven't got a fingerprint yet. I was hoping that we'd get a footprint of the running shoe. There are a lot of things to be itemized for the insurance company. I have to fill out triplicate copies and all that endless paperwork."

"We could use some fresh coffee for inspiration." Clancy dug into his trouser pocket, fishing out a loonie and a toonie. "Easy come, easy go. Do you want to hop down to Apple Annie's and bring us back some? You might get some ideas on your way there."

"You treat me like a glorified gofer," said Greg, straightening his shoulders. "I'm a police officer, not a gofer."

"Well, David and I are working on an important murder case. Murder comes first. Don't be so sensitive, so touchy, Greg. You're getting fresh air, not breathing in the stale air of the office."

Greg slowly got up from his desk, but not before giving Clancy a dirty look. As he left, he slammed the door.

"Touchy, touchy," murmured Clancy

***

Clancy walked back to the office and over to David's desk. "Now that we have got the victim's name and the name of the temp agency she worked for, I got the names of her parents and where they live, on a farm outside of Coldwater. First, I should put in a call to make sure that they are home. David, you're a sensitive soul, you go and handle the interview."

David grimaced. This was one task as a police officer he hated doing telling the grief-stricken parents.

Chapter 18

David drove up Highway 12 from Mariposa to Coldwater and then looked for a farm off the concession road with the name 'Love' on the mailbox. Finally, he found it.

He drove in along a dusty road, flanked by tall poplar trees, to a two storey, plain brick farmhouse. Not far away was a red barn with a weathervane on its roof. There were several silver milk churns lined up at the sidestep of the house waiting to be collected.

This was going to be very difficult, David thought, telling the parents that their much-loved daughter had been murdered.

A very pretty garden of geraniums, asters and marigolds grew around the verandah.

He slowly walked up the wooden steps to the front door and knocked on the screen door. He knocked again. From across a plowed field to his left, a figure was running towards him. It was a middle-aged woman in jeans and sports shirt, a blue bandana covered her hair.

She waved and called out to him, "Hello. Hello. How can I help you?"

He asked if they could find a comfortable place to sit down.

"We got your telephone call half hour ago. It has made us very anxious. It's not often we get visitors during the day like this."

"I'm afraid I have some bad news for you and your husband," said David.

"What on earth is it?" she said, when she'd settled herself into a chair on the verandah. David made it as simple and direct as possible. "Your daughter, Debbie Love is dead."

"What? It can't be," Mrs. Love's face became flushed. She

shook her head.

"Your daughter was murdered."

"Oh no, that's impossible. She was here at the farmhouse a few days ago visiting. Then a friend picked her up before supper in his car."

"Did she say who her friend was?"

"No."

"Did you get a chance to see that person when he drove up?"

"No. She walked down the lane to the highway and waited. I didn't think it was a good idea, A gentleman would have come to the house, met us, her parents and then picked her up. But she insisted and off she went."

David pressed on. "She was found in Reg Law's trunk. He was a married lawyer practicing in Mariposa. Have you ever heard her mention his name or that she was associating with him?"

"No, never. Debbie didn't go out with married men. Her father wouldn't put up with that."

"Did she live here? Or did she have an apartment in Mariposa? We will need to interview the people she lived with."

"Several months ago, she moved to share a flat with a girl friend there. I can give you the address. It's on Laclie Street."

"We will need somebody to come and identify the body. Is your husband available?"

"Yes, he's out in the barn next door. I'll get him." Mrs. Love was breathing heavily. She got up and sat down again in the chair trying to get her breath. "The shock, it's such a shock."

Mr. Love came out of the barn. "My wife tells me that they found Debbie's body in some lawyer's car in the parking lot up at Port Severn. Debbie never went out with married men. Debbie was a good girl.

"She went out on a date that night, but I didn't get to meet the gentleman. I should have insisted. This all could have been prevented. I'm a pretty good judge of character." He put his head in his hands. "This is such a shock." Then, looking up at David, he asked, "How did she get there? Any idea? "

"At this point in time, Mr. Love, we are as much in the dark as you are."

"Right now, we need a positive identification from you. Will you come with me down to the morgue and identify your daughter?"

"Give me a few minutes and I'll change out of my work clothes."

David sat with Mrs. Love, who was quietly weeping, while

Mr. Love went inside to change. David felt sorry for them, hard working, honest farm people, they didn't deserve this tragedy in their lives. Mr. Love came out of the house wearing an ill-fitting black suit, blue tie and hat. He nodded at David.

He was silent on the drive all the way into Mariposa. David drove into the parking lot of Soldiers Memorial Hospital and parked.

They walked to the front door and then down the stairs to the morgue. It was faster than waiting to take the elevator. In the morgue office, David found Mel Hat sitting at a small desk. "We need a viewing for identification purposes. Please bring out the body of the young woman found yesterday."

It took a few minutes before the curtain opened and there lay before them the cold body of Debbie Love, a pretty girl even in death, partly covered by a white sheet.

"Yes, that's her. That's my little girl. How can this be?" sobbed Mr. Love. "I don't understand this at all. My other daughter ran off a year ago to Toronto and we haven't heard from her since. I'll have to get in touch with her and tell her. Life is so cruel." He buried his head in his hands and wept. David waited for him to stop.

"Thank you, Mr. Love. After they do an autopsy, the body will be released to you for burial. It may take a few days."

"Yes, yes, I understand and yet it's all beyond my comprehension," said Mr. Love."

"I'll give you a ride back to your farm."

"Thank you, there are things I've got to do. The relatives must be told, and arrangements made when the time comes."

***

Clancy was quite sure that Debbie Love was the same woman in the restaurant with Reg Law, but he wanted a positive identification. So, he drove up again to the Riverhouse Restaurant. He was coming this way so often that he remembered each passing farmhouse along the way.

He found June, the young waitress whom he had spoken to before, on the patio serving drinks. It was a sunny day and there were several couples under the umbrellas enjoying themselves. They smiled at him in greeting as he walked by. He sat down at an empty table and waved to June to come over.

"We talked earlier in the week. I want to show you another photo." He took out the photo. "Is this the young woman who came to dinner with Reg Law several nights ago?"

She picked it up and studied it. "Could be. It looks like her. I wasn't looking at her too carefully. Yes, it's a close resemblance."

"Her name is Debbie Love; she has been found murdered."

"Oh," gasped June, "she ate dinner here that night that it happened?"

"Yes," said Clancy nodding his head.

"It's hard to believe it. Poor thing, too young to die," said June and shook her head.

"Did they mention where they were going when they left the restaurant? Did they mention any plans? Any places?"

"No, I didn't overhear their conversation. I was too busy waiting on other tables."

Clancy thanked her and put the photo away.

Chapter 19.

The day so far had been depressing, a young woman had been brutally murdered by person unknown. Clancy sat back in his swivel chair and put his feet up on his desk mulling things over. While he was thinking over the murders and the robbery an old geezer in long loopy trousers held up by red suspenders poked his way into the office. A shock of white hair framed two large black eyes, a pointed beak of a nose and a long chin that jutted out indignantly. "I'm here to report an infraction of the LCBO liquor license down at Brewery Bay pub."

"Oh," said Clancy now interested in what he was going to say. "What's your name?"

"Horace Dithers." He snapped his red suspenders once, then twice.

"What can I do for you?"

"I was sitting in a corner, at the end of the bar, nursing my beer the other night minding my own business, of trouble to no one. I was out for a quiet evening A young woman in her twenties came in and sat down next to me. She was talking loudly to her companion. I asked her to tone it down. Several times I turned to her and I asked her very politely to lower her voice. I couldn't hear myself think above the noise.

"Then she turned to me, lifted up her T-shirt, exposing herself showing her big knockers, shaking them loosely in my face, an inch from my nose. She said, "What's your problem, pop?"

"How disgusting. I waved to the manager and called him over. I said, did you see that? This is diabolical. Where are your standards? This is below the standards of decency."

"See what?' the manager said when he walked over to me. I didn't see anything, Pop.' Meanwhile, the young woman had pulled her shirt down.

"I couldn't believe it, such behavior, public exposure of breasts in a nice established bar. They could lose their license. I urged the manager to take down details, but he wouldn't. He said he couldn't find a pen or a pencil. I didn't have one on me or I would have lent him mine.

"On my own time, and with great effort, I have come down to the police station to report this and have my complaint formally recorded. If this happens again, I hope they lose their license."

"There is just one problem, Mr. Dithers, it's a case of she said, you said. Your word against hers. Have you got any witnesses to this event?"

"The whole bar."

"Name one person."

Mr. Dithers sighed, "I don't think anyone saw this spectacle but me. It happened in a corner in the rear of the bar It was kind of dark."

"I see," said Clancy. "Well Mr. Dithers, I've got two murders to solve. You're taking up my time." He shuffled some papers. "Good day." Privately, he thought Pop was lucky to get an eyeful of young flesh at his age without having to pay for it.

"There isn't any justice," replied Mr. Dithers stomping off.

Chapter 20

"Another day, another autopsy, not like Toronto where they do up to four or more a day, so many black men are murdering each other," mused Dr. Frost, "Very little happens in Mariposa, but this time it's for Debbie Love."

As far as Clancy was concerned, Dr. Frost was a real cold fish. He had gone to Western University and had played on the football team in his undergrad and graduate years before graduating in medicine. Then he chose his specialty, cutting up dead bodies.

Dr. Frost lived a quiet life in the suburbs of Mariposa with his wife. Clancy had been invited the odd timer to his house for wine and cheese, which had been pleasant. Perhaps another invite was in the offering after the autopsy?

Suited up and ready, Clancy looked down at the cold female body, looking like a Greek marble statue, on the steel gurney in front of him, her head of curls resting on a steel block. He felt regret at this terrible waste, so young for her to have come to this unlikely end.

"Well let us begin," said Dr. Frost crisply. "No lingering thoughts."

Mel Hat turned on the overhead light and the fan, which whirled above. Like ghostly figures in scrubs, booties and head gear, Clancy, Mel Hat and Dr. Frost solemnly took up their positions around the steel table.

Dr. Frost reached up for the ultraviolet lamp and went swiftly over her body, hoping to pick up hair strands, fibers, paint, or anything that could be used as evidence. Nothing came up.

Then he lifted her head, feeling for bumps, turning it from

side to side, exposing the bruises on either side of the throat and the chin.

"See this large thumb print? We need to take a photo of that with the laser. It looks like it belongs to a man by the size of it. The horse shaped hyoid bone at the base of the neck is broken. It looks like she was strangled.

"I am going to look for other bruises on her body and then check the fingernails to see if she put up a struggle. I need to find skin or blood for DNA purposes."

"How do you think it happened?" asked Clancy.

"Her assailant knelt on her forearms, see where the bruising is, also the centre of her chest." He pointed to an indentation. "After he raped her, he strangled her.

"Let's check the genital area. I will take some swabs of her vagina and see what comes up. Bruising in the vagina indicates she was alive when she was raped. Our murderer was very rough and very violent."

Dr. Frost made a quick survey of her body, looking at the skin for bruises, puncture wounds, on her ankles or hands for any additional damage. He noted the tiny butterfly tattoo on her shoulder and an old scar tissue from a burn on her right arm. Her face had a small birthmark on the forehead between the eyes.

Then, Dr. Frost took a large sharp knife and made the Y incision down her chest, exposing the rib cage. Next, he took a saw to snap open the rib cage, taking out the heart and the lungs, the liver, the intestines and the pancreas. They had to be weighed and checked for bleeding and abnormalities. Clancy always hated the whirring sound of the saw cutting into bone. It reminded him of the dentist's chair.

"So far it looks like she was a healthy 28-year-old female, in the prime of life."

With everything weighed and her body examined, the autopsy was over. Mel Hat, the morgue technician quickly sewed up the body cavity so it could be released to the next of kin and funeral arrangements could be made.

The cause of death, Dr. Frost wrote, Debbie Love had been strangled with a great deal of force, presumably by a male.

When they were changing out of their scrubs, Dr. Frost popped the question. "Clancy drop around for some wine and cheese at Happy Hour, we can shoot the breeze on my back patio. I'll phone and tell the wife you're coming."

Clancy was really a beer man but saying no to Dr. Frost

wasn't smart politics. One glass of wine wouldn't kill him and then he could make his excuses to not stay long.

Promptly at five o'clock, Clancy parked his car in front of Dr. Frost's house, an attractive two-storey brick house with wide bay windows and a rear garden backing onto Lake Couchiching. There were so many attractively built houses on the drive along the lake that this one didn't stand out. All were more than he could possibly afford.

Dr. Frost was waiting on the flagstone patio at the rear of the house, wearing dark sunglasses, a baseball cap, T-shirt and Bermuda shorts.

"Good to see, you, Clancy. Pull up a chair and rest your feet. Red or white? I have a nice Chardonnay cooling, or a deep Burgundy?"

"White sounds good."

Clancy settled back in his Muskoka chair to enjoy the view of the waterfront, the white swans and the mallards swimming by with their little yellow goslings trailing behind. It would have been picture perfect except for the presence of Dr. Frost.

"As a coroner I find it very interesting about that homicidal nurse down in Woodstock. Have you read about it in the papers, Clancy? She's accused of having killed eight seniors and assaulted many more."

"Yeh, the headlines caught my attention."

"She blabbed the details to her therapist or her psychiatrist at CAMH during her drug treatment program. They haven't said who she confessed to, just someone at CamH. Conversations with therapists are supposed to be kept confidential which is probably why they haven't named anyone. The therapist called the police.

"If she hadn't blabbed, what would have stopped her? No one would have been the wiser and she might have gone on to killing more. That was what was so scary about the whole situation. There were no checks in place."

Clancy nodded. "I read that when they arrested her, there had been no mention of a court order to exhume any patient bodies, which indicated to me that there was no incriminating substance, no deadly drug to be found there,"

"I can understand that. Some of her patients had been embalmed, some cremated, etc. There was no point. So, my question was what drug was used to be lethal and hard to detect? She confessed to injecting them with insulin."

"Insulin used for the treatment of diabetes?" asked Clancy

"Yes, as a coroner I would have difficulty pinpointing the cause of death because insulin is very hard to detect in the body after death. Overdoses of insulin do not remain in the body.

"She is alleged to have given her patients high doses of insulin which eventually rendered them unconscious. With a high dose of insulin, the body releases a high dose of adrenalin. For those with heart problems their heart goes into irregular rhythms, followed by heart attacks.

"If the patient is alive, the best thing to do is to check the blood sugar level and if found to be low, give the patient glucose. But in sick, elderly patients some already have low blood sugars, not due to insulin, but to illness. If you're not looking for it, you'll miss it.

"It's going to be a hard case to prosecute because the police have got to find her signature for signing out for the use of the drug, the dates and the times. If she didn't sign, then there will be more difficulties for the prosecution. Her defense, of course, will be that she was on drugs and didn't know what she was doing."

"It sounds difficult to prosecute," replied Clancy

"Ah, but the word on the grapevine is that she might plead guilty as charged, which would save having the time and costs of a trial. She would receive the maximum penalty, life imprisonment. Hopefully, she'll never again see the light of day."

"What is going on in seniors' homes is really criminal. Male patients beating to death old ladies etc. Something's got to be done." said Clancy

"You can say that again." Dr. Frost raised his glass. "Well, here's to summer and good times ahead."

Chapter 21

In the quiet of the office, Clancy turned things over in his mind. An angry wasp was buzzing at the window trying to get in, no chance. Someone must know what has been going on between Reg Law and Debbie Love. What does Mrs. Law have to say? She must know something. She must have suspected something. He was not satisfied with her earlier answers.

Clancy drove again up to the Law house. The living room curtains were drawn. The house looked forlorn and empty. Clancy buzzed, setting off the chimes. He waited. The intercom came on, "Who's there?"

"Sergeant Clancy of the OPP."

Mrs. Law, in flats and jeans, came to the door. She didn't look so happy to see him.

"Can we find a place to sit down? I have some serious questions to ask you." She led him into the living room, where an empty coffee mug sat on a glass coffee table beside the day's newspaper and a pile of opened mail. Bills to pay?

"Mrs. Law," said Clancy," I've been making inquiries and it seems that the waitress at the Riverside Restaurant identifies Debbie Love as the female guest of your husband. I showed her Debbie's photo, the same one I showed you. She said that they both came in for dinner that night around seven and left around nine pm. In the past, apparently several times, Debbie has eaten there with him."

"That's hard to believe. I don't understand this at all. My husband was there with a young woman? Is she sure that it was him there? I don't believe that my husband would carry on behind my back like this."

"You said that you'd never seen her before when I showed you that picture." Clancy stared at her hard.

"Yes," said Mrs. Law quietly, lowering her gaze, her lip quivering, "I told you the truth. I didn't lie to you."

"Did you know your husband was having an affair with the office temp? That could be a motive for murder."

She shook her head. "I trusted my husband in all things. He would never do that."

"Well, it seems that he was having an affair with Debbie Love. Did he mention that he wanted a divorce or intended to leave your marriage?"

"Not in the least. Never." Mrs. Law shook her head firmly.

"I have made a record of your remarks, Mrs. Law. I hope that they're accurate and that I don't find out later that it's all been a big lie." Clancy got up to go. "Don't make any travel plans." Mrs. Law looked grim. He let himself out.

Chapter 22

He went back to the office and shared his suspicions with David. The phone rang.
"It's Mr. Love on the phone, he wants to give a message to someone." called out Greg, who was interrupted in pursuit of a big black cockroach skittering its way across the floor, probably after some doughnut crumbs.
"I'll take it," said David.
"I want to tell you that the visitation for my daughter, Debbie, will take place on Friday afternoon from 3 to 5 p.m. The funeral will be held on Saturday at 11 a.m. at Hunter Funeral home, on the main street of Coldwater," said Mr. Love.
"Thank you for telling us," said David, calling out to Clancy "If you want, I'll go myself and save you the trouble of going,"
"Great. That would save me a trip," said Clancy

***

The next day, Saturday, David drove up an hour early to the funeral home, giving him plenty of time to peruse the scene and look for anyone out of place.
It was a dismal day, one minute with sheets of rain pouring down, clearing, then raining again, weather a duck would love. The highway was wet and slippery. He had to drive carefully. The countryside was enveloped in a heavy grey mist with shadows of trees and bushes in the background.
He easily found the Hunter Funeral Home, on the main street, a large red brick Victorian mansion, with several chimneys

on its roof. In front of the garage was parked a large black hearse. The front part of the house had been converted into a funeral home. David climbed the carpeted stone steps.

Inside in the hall, a sign over an open door said, 'Room 1, Debbie Love'. David signed the visitation book.

Debbie Love's coffin was at the far end of the room. David walked slowly towards it. He paused in front of the coffin looking down at a pretty young woman who had been violently raped and murdered.

What a waste of a young life!

Three years ago, he had looked down at his wife lying in her coffin. The pain was still there from the memory and the fact that she had been taken in childbirth, an embolism had shortened her life. Time heals all wounds they say but he still felt the pain of loss. He had to keep busy and not dwell on her death. He still missed her. It was hard not to.

Debbie lay on a bed of white satin ruffles. Her head, with her brown curls, on a satin white pillow. A white lace band hid the purple strangulation marks around her throat. Like a virginal bride, she was wearing a white lace dress with a modest scooped neckline. Her hands were clasped holding a gold cross and a Bible.

David shook his head, thinking about the utter waste of it all. Then headed over to glance at the flowers and their tags. A large bouquet of red roses was from Gary Potts. *I will love you forever.* Was this her boyfriend? A carnation arrangement was from Mr. and Mrs. Henry Love, probably her grandparents. Several other bouquets in large vases were placed next to them with one from Patty Blake, her roommate.

He walked over to look at the photos of Debbie's life arranged in a photo gallery. Pictures of Debbie as a cute young baby; in kindergarten with her class and then grade school. Outside of school she had become a member of Brownies, then Girl Guides. In High School, she joined the 4 H club. There were graduation pictures with her peers. A nice one showed Debbie in her pink formal before the prom. There were pictures of her milking a cow, collecting eggs on the farm, feeding the horses. Pictures with her sister and her family, nothing that would predict this violent ending.

David heard voices. It was her young friends from school filing in. He looked at the faces, trying to find a face that did not fit in. But could not.

It was time for him to take a seat at the back of the chapel. There were few older people. The last persons to enter were Debbie

Love's parents who went and sat in the front row.

The minister, in long flowing white robe came and stood at the dais. "Let us bow our heads in prayer. We ask the Lord for strength in this dark hour."

On a printed program, with a picture of Debbie on the cover was the hymn, *Be Thou My Vision, My Strength and My Light.*

When they had finished singing, the minister gestured for them to be seated.

He began his homily.

"Bad things happen to good people, for which there is no answer. We condemn the violence of this act that took the life of Debbie Love. Why this happened, we don't know. Life is a mystery in which only God knows the answers. In these sad times, remember the words of the Lord, *I go to prepare a place for you. In my house are many rooms.*"

He spoke for about fifteen minutes, then a hymn, *Abide with Me* was sung, followed by a prayer for the soul of Debbie Love. The service was over.

The curtains were drawn. When they swung open again, the casket was closed. The funeral director and his aides dressed in black mourning suits entered and wheeled the casket out of the room towards the waiting hearse followed by her grief stricken parents, who got up and walked slowly down the aisle with their heads bowed , others following row after row silently behind them.

The rain was still pouring down as David walked down the steps and headed hurriedly for his car in the parking lot. It was all so depressing, the rain and the funeral. He decided to skip the visit to the local cemetery where she would be buried. Nothing more could be added to the investigation at this point. He decided to head into Apple Annie's when he got back to town, a more cheerful spot.

When he looked around the restaurant, he saw all the tables were full. Where would he sit? He recognized Mrs. Sandy, sitting alone at her table. "Mind if I join you?" he asked.

"With pleasure," said Mrs. Sandy. smiling. "I just got an email from the Mariposa Historic Society with the good news about the S.S. Keewatin, the only Edwardian steamship still surviving in the world. The dock at Port McNicholl is being rebuilt and landscaped to accommodate it."

"Oh, that's interesting," said David.

"It's 109 years old, weighs 4,000 tons. It used to carry over 1,600 tonnes of grain on the Great Lakes to Port McNicholl. It also took immigrants and their families, animals and farm equipment and moved them up the Great Lakes. They docked at Fort William, now Thunder Bay. From there they would take the trains west to their farmlands.

"It's a time capsule of Canadian History. The federal government gave $480,000.00 for the new dock and landscape. Imagine that?" said Mrs. Sandy. "Now, how, are things going with you? Any luck with solving the murders?"

"Without saying too much, it's hard to tell if they were targeted or if it was a random act of violence, them being in the wrong place at the wrong time. It will take some sorting out. Any suggestions?"

"Offhand, I have no idea. Reg Law was a respected lawyer in the community and, as for the girl, I've heard nothing. It's quite a scandal."

"Give us a ring if you hear anything, no matter how trivial it might be," said David getting up. "Got to get back to the mine and heave coal."

"Take care," she laughed. "Goodbye."

David walked along the street, looking into the windows of the shops. Then he noticed a woman with pepper coloured hair, a slight figure dressed in a flowery gathered skirt and sandals. Despite the sunglasses, he recognized her. Mildred Lemon, the former librarian assistant who quit to find a happier life away from her overbearing boss at the library, Mrs. Proudfoot.

"Mildred, hello. Good to see you. How are you getting on? Where are you working now?"

"Quite nicely, thank you. My life now is like a breath of freedom. I am working at the Neighbourhood Legal Aid Clinic as an intake worker. I quite enjoy it, a pleasant office."

"You caught me staring at a pretty dress in the window and I was trying to make a decision and now I have. Go for it!"

"Good for you, Mildred. Glad things worked out so well."

"I just needed a little push."

"Don't we all." David left her to continue down the street to the office.

Chapter 23

When Clancy had shown Debbie Love's picture to the office secretary, Miss Neat, and pressed for further details of her personal life, he hadn't got much information. Debbie Love, according to her, lived on Brant street, in an upstairs apartment. Clancy sent David over to check it out. "See if anyone is there."

David drove up to the house and parked.

It was a two-storey, brick house, rather plain with a grass yard in front. Blue and green garbage bins stood at the curb. Two women's bicycles were chained to the wooden veranda posts, along with two wicker chairs with cushions. A wicker plant stand held a large fern.

There were two bell knobs on the side of the door, but he couldn't read the writing, He tried the lower one. An old lady peered out of the front window and shook her fist at him, mouthing, 'Go away.' He tried the top one. The buzzer sounded. The door opened. He walked along the wooden floor of the hall, then headed up the stairs at the far end.

A young woman in jeans and a pink T-shirt, with a bandana holding her brown hair back, was standing at the top waiting for him.

She extended her hand. On her arm were silver bracelets. "Hello, I'm Patty Blake, how can I help you?"

"I've come to make inquiries about the murder of your flat-mate. Is there a place we can sit down?"

"Yes, of course, follow me." She led him into the living room, which had a sofa and two chairs. A record player sat on a small table. David waited for her to sit down, then sat down himself.

"What can you tell me about Debbie's disappearance?"

Patty took a sip of water then dabbed at her eyes. "When she didn't come home that night, I just assumed she was on a date. I didn't think anything of it." She took another sip of water. "Can you tell me a few details."

David nodded. "She was found in the trunk of a car."

Patty shook her head. Tears streamed down her face." My best friend. This is awful. You were lucky, you caught me. I'm a yoga instructor at the Y. I teach classes this afternoon."

"What was Debbie like?"

"Very pleasant, nice to be around."

"What was her job?"

"She worked as an office temp, on a part time basis. Sometimes there was not that much work."

"She was short of cash?"

"Yes, she was often late with the rent and the groceries. We're in a recession. There's not that much work around."

"How long have you known Debbie?"

"We went to high school together. Best friends. When we left home, we decided to rent a flat together."

"Her family, what can you tell me about them?"

"They lived up on a farm near Coldwater. The farm was basically for raising cattle, livestock. It wasn't a place for a girl. Debbie didn't want to stay on the farm. She wanted to leave it all behind."

"Did she get along with her parents?"

"With her mom, yes, her dad was strict, old fashioned, not fun loving like Debbie. They clashed."

"Did she have a boyfriend?"

"She had one. He was a bit rough around the edges. He worked in construction. I felt he couldn't give Debbie the things that she needed.

"He was a beer and nuts sort of guy, football Saturday afternoon on the TV, pizza for supper, Chinese take-out, that sort of thing. They never seemed to go anywhere, just popping the popcorn and ordering in pizza. I felt that she could do a lot better. Go places, go out for dinner, go dancing, go to concerts, that sort of thing."

"What was his name?" asked David.

"Gary Potts. Lately she seemed to be seeing someone else and not Gary."

"Oh, that's interesting. Did she break up with Gary?"

"Not in so many ways, just a slow cooling off, not seeing him as frequently. I sensed she was seeing someone else on the side. She never brought him back here or introduced me to him. She was very secretive about him. Never mentioned his name. She'd meet him after work at the bar or various places they went to, it was all hush, hush. I figured that he was married."

"Did you have any idea of who he was? His name?"

She shook her head.

"Where can I find this Gary Potts?"

"He's probably working, but he hangs out after work at Brewery Bay some evenings. You could catch him there or at the Y."

"If you can think of anything else, let me know. Here's my card," said David getting up to leave.

Chapter 24.

　　Clancy nodded at David as he came in. Greg was standing in front of Clancy's desk. "I want no interruptions, Greg, I have to concentrate. I don't care if the coffee machine broke down. Buy another. Don't bother me with the details. Yes, it comes out of petty cash. Not my pocket. Speaking of which, where's the water delivery truck with distilled water for our cooler. It's running low. Can you give them a call?"
　　Greg gave him a dirty look.
　　Clancy chewed on his ball point pen, deep in thought.
　　His best guess, as to the friend who picked Debbie up on the highway outside her parents' place that night, was Reg Law who arranged to meet her and take her to dinner. As a married man, he would have all kinds of excuses for not driving in and meeting her parents especially if they would ask questions and were strict about who their daughter was seeing. They wouldn't want their daughter going out with a married man. Reg could have told Debbie that he worked late at the office, that it was important for him not to be seen around town with a woman, other than his wife. It would be bad for his reputation. Clancy figured that Law, might not have had a happy marriage but it was a stable relationship with his wife, and he was not going to risk it by being seen with Debbie.
　　Debbie Love's body was found in the trunk of his car and Reg Law was found in the lake. Could they assume that both died at roughly the same time?
　　Law dined with Debbie at the Riverhouse Restaurant, which was confirmed by the waitress. What happened afterwards? Where did they go from there? They had at least two hours ahead of them

before Law was killed and presumably Debbie.

Did they park at the Headlands near the locks where the car was found? There seems to be only one set of tire tracks, but the rain could have washed away any sign of others.

***

While Clancy was ruminating, making circles on a piece of paper in front of him. Bob White, the homicide detective from head office, popped his head around the door. He sniffed the air. "I smell apple cores, banana skins and coffee. Open a window and let fresh air in. This place smells like a garbage can."

Clancy blushed and went to open a window. How insulting. They'd have to be more vigilant.

"How are the murder cases going? What have you got for me?"

"It's all speculation. My guess is that Reg Law and Debbie Love were parked right where they were killed. It was a lovely warm evening, with a blue sky and sunset not until eight. The lake would have been flat and calm. They were probably making out. There was one sample of semen collected from Debbie's vagina. Reg Law's.

"Was it a random or did the assailant have some connection to Law or Debbie? How did he know they were there? Had anyone seen that car parked there before? Tim, the young boy who found Reg Law's body might have seen them when he went fishing.

"You'll have to pursue all lines of inquiry. Search the data base for recent sexual assaults and violent rapes. The Crown will want to know if we've done that when we present our case for conviction."

"I'll get right on it," replied Clancy. "Good thinking." Bob White gave a last look around the room, gave a sniff and then shut the door.

There were a lot of domestic cases, that involved violence, husbands beating up wives, but few of wives attacking their husbands in the police data base.

There was one a violent rape, on a jogging trail outside of Barrie, close enough to be interesting. Rick Thorn, age 28, had just spent four years in Kingston pen and had been released on probation, after serving his sentence for the crime.

Clancy phoned to the OPP in Barrie and got the duty desk. "Can someone there give me some info on the Rick Thorn rape and assault case that happened about four years ago?"

"I'll put you through to the detectives' offices."

He was buzzed through.

"Your lucky day," said Colin Fey, "I remember him well. I was the chief arresting officer. Here are the details.

"On a hot day, a young woman in shorts and halter was jogging along a trail, north of here. Rick Thorn had hidden in the bushes nearby. When she jogged past him, he leaped out and grabbed her, hauling her into the bushes. He tore off her clothes, put his hand over her mouth and said he would kill her if she yelled. Then he violently raped her, leaving the young woman covered in bruises, with a black eye and a broken arm. She gave the police a good description of him, and not long afterwards, a cruiser spotted him on the street in downtown Barrie, coming out of a bar and he was promptly arrested.

"His previous conviction was for sexual assault on a young female high school student for which he got three years. Fortunately, she had managed to escape without serious injuries.

"If you read through the case on file, it tells of his childhood, violent beatings by his father who had uncontrolled rages. The family dog was kicked to death by his father. His mother was beaten many times by his father in front of him. This had all contributed to turn him into a violent adult. We'll be seeing more of Rick Thorn before he reaches the pearly gates. We have to keep an eye on him."

"Thanks for your help."

This looks like a very good suspect, thought Clancy. I've got to check it out. So, he drove down to Barrie, a good twenty-minute drive away, to find Rick Thorn and interview him. The Parole Office had given him the address and phone number. Why phone ahead? He wanted to surprise him.

Rick Thorn was living in a halfway house in a sketchy part of town. It was a run-down rooming house, with six blue garbage bins stacked side by side on the sidewalk. The trim on the house needed paint and the brickwork was chipped in places. Sitting on the wooden verandah, were two rough looking men, smoking. A third was standing, leaning against a post. Clancy drove into the driveway.

"Any of you Rick Thorn?"

"Why do you want to know?" asked the tall man in T-shirt and jeans who was leaning against the post.

"I want to have a little chat with him."

'Yeh, friendly chat, huh? I'm Rick Thorn. What do you want?" He stared at Clancy.

"Something has come up."

"Yeh, like what?"

"Have you been in the vicinity of Port Severn locks lately? There's been a violent rape and murder up in that area."

"No and how would I get there? I have no means of transportation. No wheels. Every time there's a violent rape or murder in the area are the police going to come by and bug me?"

"You have a rap sheet. How do you get around?" asked Clancy.

"Take the bus like everyone else."

"What time is your curfew?"

"Nine o'clock."

Time wise, Clancy thought, that was a short window of opportunity, but it was still possible. If he got a ride, he could hitch hike there and back and meet his curfew. The autopsy report said around nine or ten the murders had taken place. There was leeway in the time the murders had been committed. Clancy wrote down his answers in his notebook.

"Got any relatives in that area?"

"Moved away when I went into the pen. No friends up there either."

I would have to find a reason for placing him there, at that time and I haven't got one yet. I need more tie- ins between him and the murders, thought Clancy.

He sighed, "We'll be in touch. I know you'll want to keep on good behavior with your parole officer."

"Yeh, a violation will send me back into the pen and that I don't want."

Clancy got into his car and drove back to Mariposa.

***

No one to check out except the names that Mel Stone had given to him from Reg Law. But Reg Law must have had other enemies, someone who wanted to kill him. My other question is who was the prime target of this attack, Reg Law or Debbie Love? thought Clancy

Is there anything to tie in Mrs. Law. She's a suspect. If she found out her husband was having an affair, she may have wanted to kill him out of jealousy and rage. But she denies knowing about the affair. Nothing points to her at this stage.

Maybe the focus should not be on who killed Reg Law but

on Debbie Love? Could a jealous boyfriend have committed the murder? Reg Law got in the way of his relationship with Debbie. He found out about Reg Law having sex with Debbie. So, my prime suspects would be the boyfriend, then anyone else that was dating her.

Clancy made a call to Forensics in Toronto about any further evidence that they might have collected on Debbie Love that might help him in the case.

Jim Morrison answered." We can't tell you much more than you already know. There were fibres from the rope that tied her ankles and her hands. This didn't tell us much. It was common garden rope, sold in any hardware store. Her skirt had grass stains on the back of it, indicating that she was dragged out of the car. The semen found in her vagina matches Reg Law's DNA. No other semen stains were found. There was extensive bruising on her thighs, as mentioned in the autopsy report and there's a nice clear fingerprint that the laser picked up on her throat which can be matched in the police data base. We found some skin under her fingernails. We checked for DNA in the police data bank. But no matches. I'm sorry, that's all we've got right now."

Clancy thanked him. The thumbprint and the DNA would help convict, but, at this stage in the game, there was more legwork to be done.

***

Clancy had stepped out on the street for a breath of fresh air, and to stretch his legs when a neat little red sports car with the top down pulled in. Clancy looked at the driver, it was Mrs. Law He hardly recognized her. Her blonde hair had been streaked and cut into a becoming pixie style. She was wearing a siren red leather jacket with lots of zippers and a short red leather miniskirt. As she got out, she flashed her long legs at him.

"Hi, there."

"Some car," said Clancy giving the car another admiring glance.

"Yes, it's part of my new lifestyle." Mrs. Law tossed her head back, "It's off with the old and on with the new. I'm putting everything behind me. The past is the past and it cannot be changed. I want to get on with my life. I'm not going to sit back and play the black widow. Life is not going to pass me by."

She pushed a strand of hair out of her eye. "I might not even have a memorial service for Reg in the fall. Instead, I could put a memorial notice in the paper. That should do. I've had him cremated and his ashes put in an urn in the garage until I find a place to scatter them. Why pay for interment? I want to keep it simple. I don't want the urn cluttering up the garage. Any developments in the murder investigations?"

"Pursuing various leads," said Clancy nonchalantly

"Let me know if you find out something."

"Sure," said Clancy. Privately he thought, over my dead body. She was a suspect and a good one at that.

Chapter 25

A blonde haired, blue eyed girl in a ponytail, wearing a pink T shirt, shorts and sneakers gave a strong knock on the door, peered around then opened it. She stood there in the doorway to Clancy's office looking very unhappy

She walked up to Clancy's desk. "My name is Claire. I've come to report a theft. My pet rabbit, Smokey, the big, black one with no spots, was stolen from his cage last night and I want a report filed with the police. I want the police to look for it."

Clancy leaned over his desk to look down at her. "How old are you, Miss?"

"Eleven."

"So, you want me to file a missing report on a black rabbit, eh? Tell me where the rabbit's cage was?"

"It was in the backyard of our house. There was a lock on the cage door which was snapped off."

"When did this happen?"

"Last night when we were all sleeping. No one heard a sound not even Stella, our dog. She didn't even bark."

"Mm," said Clancy, deep in thought. "Have any older boys from your school come over to your house to admire your rabbit or taken an interest in it?"

"When people come over to play, or have a swim, we have a pool, I show them my rabbit," said Claire

"What is the value of your rabbit, in dollars and cents?"

"Very valuable. I bought it for $35 at the fall country fair."

"I see, so its theft under $100.00," said Clancy, slowly getting to his feet and putting his hands on his hips. "Well Claire, we have limited police resources here, we're short of manpower. I don't see how we can be much help. You will have to play detective. It's up to you to figure out who may have taken it, then go around to their houses. Look in their backyards. Then come back and report to me and we'll see what we can do."

"I thought the police were paid to help people find stolen things, to catch thieves."

"Some things," said Clancy gravely, stroking his chin, "but not all."

"You don't care about my stolen rabbit," yelled Claire. "You're no help at all. My dad's a teacher. He works hard to pay your salary. He pays taxes. You won't lift a finger." She stomped out of the office.

One unsatisfied customer, but we can't please them all. I didn't want to tell her that we don't chase thefts under $100.00. Nor do we chase missing rabbits, thought Clancy.

His phone began ringing. He looked at the number. Bob White. Sod that. It would have to wait. The answering machine would pick it up.

***

At the same time Claire stomped out, frail old Miss Temple, dressed in her usual black dress and shawl, staggered through the door clutching her head. "I'm going blind," she cried. "The wind blew something into my eye just now. I can't see. I was out shopping, and this had to happen. I'm going blind. Where's a chair?" she squeaked.

Clancy groaned and pulled one up in front of his desk, "Here's one. Sit down here, Miss Temple. Let me see your eye and see what the trouble is. Roll your eyes to the left, now to the right.'

He looked at her red rimmed eyeball but could see nothing.

"Shed a few tears, Miss Temple and this will clear your eye. Have you a handkerchief?"

"Of course, I have one. No respectable person goes out on the street these days without one in their handbag."

Clancy said, "I could wet it for you, and you could dab the corner in your eye." He went to the washroom and taking a corner of the handkerchief, ran it under the cold-water tap. He returned and gave it to Miss Temple. She took it and dabbed at her eye.

He waited. Miss Temple became calmer. She sighed and let a tear roll down her cheek. Then she opened the affected eye. "It's gone, thank heavens, thank the Lord for that. I need to rest for a few minutes. Collect my thoughts."

Rest? Why can't she rest at home? Why here?

Clancy heaved a big sigh. He had two murders to solve. He needed to concentrate. How could he concentrate when a ten-year-old girl wanted him to find her stolen rabbit and an old lady wanted to sit down for a rest in the office chair for half an hour? The public was driving him crazy. Who would come through the door next?

He snapped a ball point pen in half, then tore up a piece of paper that he had been writing a report on, too many spelling mistakes. His phone began ringing. He ignored it.

Finally, Miss Temple got slowly to her feet and thanked him for helping her, "A friend in need is a friend indeed," she exclaimed.

Clancy said nothing. Silence was golden. He was afraid of what he might say. Diplomacy wasn't his longest suit.

***

When the office was finally cleared of its visitor, Greg's head popped around the door. "You remembered that hippy who used to walk his dog past our office, pausing to let the dog pee on the fire hydrant. It was his form of protest. He stopped for a while, but now he's taken to doing it again every morning. Where I sit next to the open window, the smell of dog pee is excruciating. I had to go down to Canadian Tire yesterday and buy Keep Off aerosol spray can again and spray the hydrant, but it doesn't work. The dog keeps lifting its leg. Can you do something about it? Otherwise, we'll have to hose down the hydrant frequently if we want to open our windows in the summer months."

"I'll have a little chat with him," said Clancy, his eyes lighting up. "Let me know when he comes by again. There are ways to deal with this."

***

The next morning, the long-haired hippy in cut-off denims, wearing a red bandana, white T shirt, and Birkenstock sandals, his dog beside him on a leather leash, sauntered down the street towards them.

"He's coming up the street now," shouted Greg, looking out of the window "Go get him, Clancy."

Clancy stood in the doorway waving his baton. The hippy

paused and looked puzzled, the dog straining on its leash.

"Don't even think it, pal," said Clancy, banging his baton against the outside wall. "Scram, and don't let me see you and that dog near the fire hydrant again or your dog will go straight to the pound."

"This is a free country. The sidewalk is free to whomever wants to walk on it. You don't own it."

"Well the fire hydrant isn't. Bugger off before I make things really interesting for you."

"We don't live in a totalitarian state," said the hippy, backing away. "I have my rights."

"Only so far, you do. Be gone. I'm running out of patience." Clancy began whacking the wooden door with big bangs. The hippy and his dog hurried down the street yelling, "Fascists!"

"I knew you could handle it," said Greg with a big smile on his face, popping his head back into the doorway. "Well done. He won't be back this way again and I won't have to keep spraying."

***

Clancy settled back in his chair to do some calculations. For once the office was quiet.

Then the office door crashed open. There was never any subtlety in Mira's entrance. "Did you see Debbie Love's photo on the front page in the Packet today?"

Clancy had read the headline: *Grisly murder at Port Severn Locks. Woman, raped, bound and gagged found in trunk of car of local lawyer, Reg Law. Abandoned car found in parking lot with smashed window.*

"Did you like it? It was a big write up. Good you say? You have an IOU Clancy and I'm here to collect."

Oh no, my wife Agnes is breathing down my neck with her 'to do' list and now payback time for Mira. "Does that mean a drink down at Brewery Bay?"

"One drink is all you offered me the last time, you cheap bastard." Mira looked at her watch. "How about lunch? I'm feeling hungry."

Clancy raised an eyebrow. "You're always hungry, Mira. How about a soup and quiche combo at Apple Annie's? I can meet you there at twelve."

"I'll accept your generous offer."

Promptly at twelve, Clancy met Mira outside the café. "Mira, find a nice table while I go stand in line for our order. The soup is Italian Wedding, thick and chunky. The quiche is mushroom and broccoli."

Coming out the door was the Reverend Billy Day in his navy blue sweat suit, out for a jog and eager to get back to the church to read he mail. He smiled and gave them a quick wave.

Over in the corner, he recognized Mrs. Sandy and old Miss Temple drinking coffee, probably hot chocolate for Miss Temple. Mrs. Barnes, an enthusiastic hiker with the Naturalist Club with legs like a goat, was sitting alone with her hiking boots on and walking sticks leaning against the wall. He wondered what birds she had spotted today.

There were several people ahead of him. Then it was his turn. Clancy put in his order then went and sat down with Mira. The young waitress brought the order to their table with two glasses of ice water.

Clancy was just taking a bite out of his quiche when he spotted Agnes coming in the door. How would he explain his presence here with Mira? Agnes didn't approve of Mira and her 'flash it and flaunt it' ways. 'A little hussy' was how she described her. The description was right on, but for professional reasons, he had to overlook it.

"Well fancy meeting you in here. I just got my hair done and was going to buy something for supper," said Agnes. She nodded at Mira. "Getting in a little nibble?"

Clancy broke in. "Mira has done us a big favour, getting the murder details reported in the Packet and Times. She's been a real help with our inquiries."

"I bet she has," hissed Agnes. "Mira is always so eager to help." Mira gave her a cold stare and continued eating.

"Sit yourself down and have a coffee with us. Have you had lunch?'

"Yes, I had mine already. I must be on my way, with things to do and more shopping. Will you be home at the usual time, Clancy? We'll have a cold supper, maybe Jell-O for dessert."

Clancy hated Jell-O, although he had a sweet tooth and craved doughnuts, cupcakes and cookies. Agnes would get her revenge, that's for sure.

"Well I must be off, enjoy yourself," said Agnes in an acidic tone that said, 'eat arsenic.'

Chapter 26

It was a great afternoon; the sun was shining. and a nice breeze was blowing off the lake. Debbie Love's roommate had given them the details on where to find Gary Potts when he was not working on a construction site. Clancy headed to the downtown Y, a tall red brick building on Peter Street. He gave his ID to the attendant, asked him where he could find Gary Potts, then pushed the turnstyle,

"In the weight room on the second floor next to the exercise room. You won't miss it."

Going to the Y made him feel guilty. Clancy knew that he should work out but finding the time was difficult. Make time, he told himself, work off that belly fat.

He passed the crowded bicycle and treadmill room One man was bending over the water fountain in the corner with several people lined up behind him.

Next, was the weight room, a large room with floor to ceiling mirrors. There was only one man working out lifting bar bells. It must be him. Gary Potts was an attractive, tall, muscular young man in his early thirties. He put down his barbells when he saw Clancy approaching.

"Gary Potts? I want to speak to you privately."

"I hope it's important because I'm in the middle of my routine."

"It's serious."

Gary raised an eyebrow. "There's a small coffee shop down on ground level. We can talk there."

Clancy found a table near the back where they wouldn't be

overheard.

When they had sat down, Clancy said, "I've come here to make inquiries. It was your girl friend, Debbie Love, who was murdered. I need some information."

"Yes, I know. I went to her funeral. It's hard to take it all in. I'm still in shock," Gary's face had turned white.

"Can you describe for me what Debbie was like?"

"She was just a nice sweet girl, no drama queen."

"When was the last time you saw her?"

"I hadn't heard from her for a couple of days, but this was not unusual. I just saw her last weekend. She was okay then." He put his head down in his hands.

Clancy waited for a few minutes, watching him, and thinking he's either a good actor or telling the truth, at this point he couldn't decide.

"How did you meet Debbie?"

"One evening I went out to the Roadhouse, on the edge of town to have a drink and take in the action. I had broken up with a previous girl friend several months back and was a bit lonely. We'd been fighting for months. Debbie was standing alone at the bar having a drink. She looked like a nice girl. I got to talking with her. I invited her to dance, took her home, then she invited me in. We started going out from that point."

"What was your relationship like with Debbie?"

"We never fought, we never quarreled unlike my previous girlfriend. It was a very steady partnership with very few highs and lows. We met on the weekends to watch movies and eat popcorn. I liked Debbie a lot."

"Were you two planning on anything permanent?"

"The financial situation was the same for me as for her, a bit dicey. I work in construction and this can be sporadic, working for several months then laid off and having to go on unemployment insurance. Debbie was an office temp, going from job to job. There wasn't a lot of security in her job or mine. So, at the moment, we couldn't plan anything for the future. I was happy the way it was. She had her place, I had mine and then we got together on the weekends. That should sum it up."

"Were you up near the Port Severn Locks recently?"

"No, I haven't been up there in years."

Lifting his head to stare at Clancy, he asked, "Do you have any idea who did this?"

"It's early days yet. We're just at the beginning of the

investigation. Have you got an alibi for several nights ago?"

"I'm usually here at the Y working out."

"Find somebody to vouch for you." said Clancy, "Give me a name."

"I will have to check around."

"Do that. We'll talk again soon. There's a lot to be gone over."

Chapter 27

With the matter of the hippy and his dog settled, Greg decided he had time to pay a courtesy call on Judge Wiffy, who had the summers off. He wanted to tell him that he was working hard on solving the robbery.

He drove to the Southwood Estate, then up the drive past the entry of stone pillars, to the front door.

When he rang the bell, he was surprised to see the portly judge greet him dressed in loose shirt, suspenders, trousers, and bedroom slippers with a coffee mug in his hand. His housekeeper had not arrived yet.

"How nice of you to make a personal call. Any results? I've been waiting to hear from you."

"Just dropped by to see how you're doing. It's hard going. Nothing yet. It all takes time."

Judge Wiffy led him into the library, the former scene of the crime, where the glass had been replaced in the bookshelves, the liquor cart cleaned up and the mess cleaned off the rugs. Greg noticed that there were still some nasty knife marks left on the cabinet doors around the locks.

"Your belongings should soon surface. The thief will want ready cash. He'll try to unload the stuff as quickly as he can."

"I should hope so. Would you care for a drink, a glass of sherry?"

"I'm not suppose to drink on the job but let's overlook it this time."

"Harvey's Shooting Sherry, only the best." Judge Wiffy walked over to the cart and poured two glasses. "Here's to catching the thief I'm very sentimental about the Leacock manuscript. I'm a great Leacock fan, especially living in Mariposa where Leacock wrote his books during his summer holidays, away from his job as professor teaching economics at McGill University.

"I love going for lunch at the Leacock Historic site, to the restaurant, overlooking Brewery Bay. I love seeing the ducks. their ducklings, and the swans swim by. On a jutting point of land is the restored boathouse where Leacock did a lot of his writing. Lunch isn't bad either. It's quiche and a salad, or soup and sandwiches, with a glass of wine. It's a friendly sort of place and you're always meeting somebody you know.

"Well here's to finding the thief." They clinked glasses.

Greg tossed back his drink in two gulps which surprised Judge Wiffy who was making his last, sipping it slowly. "Got to go but will keep you posted," said Greg.

"Do that."

Greg decided that it was well worth visiting Judge Wiffy and he would call in again to keep him up to date. The glass of sherry was a nice bonus.

Chapter 28

The heat in the office was stifling. Clancy turned on the overhead fan then sat down at his. Greg looked over at him.

"I need your help, Clancy. I'm in a quandary. Where would someone unload the first edition of a book? There are no rare bookstores here in Mariposa, or in Barrie for that matter. There's no market for them. How would our thief contact a buyer?

"If a notice has been put out in the social media that the book has been stolen it would be hard to unload it for a good price down in Toronto where most of the rare book dealers are. Where should I look?" asked Greg.

"Easy," said Clancy, "try eBay."

"Will do."

On eBay Greg typed the word 'manuscripts' in the search window then hit the return key. Over 1700 manuscripts immediately popped up. It will take several hours to find it if it's here, he thought.

He slowly scrolled down the screen, pausing at each listed manuscript psalms on medieval vellum; antique Islamic documents, Beatrice Potter's 'Taylor of Gloucester'; original Latin Bible; ancient Talmudic writings and Turkish Korans; palm leaf and vellum manuscripts and an Ethiopian Coptic Bible.

There was a lot of fascinating stuff listed. To cut to the chase, he refined his search by typing in the search window, first editions. He scrolled down. He hadn't been looking long before, finally, there it was. To his surprise it was listed. '1st Edition. *Leacock's Sunshine Sketches of a Little Town.*'

Bingo!

He got the seller's email, phone number and the shipping address. What a dummy the thief was, he thought, to post it on eBay. He must be desperate thinking the police wouldn't look there.

But his search wasn't over yet. Greg got into his car and drove south of Mariposa to Medonte's county roads, farmland on either side of the highway.

He drove up to a plain red brick farmhouse on the edge of Mariposa. He knocked on the door. An old farmer in black wellington boots, jeans and rumpled leather jacket came to the door. Not the kind of thief that he'd imagined. He thought it was unlikely that this old farmer would break into Judge Wiffy's house. It had to be someone younger. Maybe it was his son who was the break and enter artist.

Greg said, "You're under arrest for selling stolen property a first edition of 'Stephen Leacock's *Sunshine Sketches of a Little Town*,' on eBay."

"What?" the farmer replied. "You're kidding me. What do you mean, it's stolen? I got it from some guy who came to the door. He was clearing out his parents' attic where he found it. He had no use for it and sold it to me cheap. I knew it was worth more, so I listed it on eBay. You've got to believe me."

Greg said, "I'll try. Do you have his name and address?"

"Come in for a few minutes and wait. I put it down on a piece of paper somewhere." He searched around in the tin box on the side table in the hall. "Yeh, here it is." He shoved the scrap of paper at Greg.

Greg looked at it. The name was probably phony as was the address. "Did you get a good look at the guy? Describe him to me."

"Dark haired, in jeans and sports jacket. About six feet tall, slim. Young, in his late twenties, early thirties."

"Any distinguishing features?"

"He had a small tattoo on his left hand, a dragon. That was all I noticed."

"Do you recall the saying anything too cheap is dear at any price."

"Yeh. From what you tell me, I'm out $25.00."

"Could have been more. The owner will be glad to get his property back."

The farmer reluctantly handed over the book, wrapped in newspaper and tied with twine.

Greg handed him his card. "If you see him again, give me a call." He took the book carefully back to his car.

Back in the car, he put in a call to Judge Wiffy. "I've got some good news to report. Your first edition has been found, safe and in good shape. I'll deliver it to your house within half an hour."

"That's wonderful news," said Judge Wiffy, "wonderful news. I was feeling a little depressed after the robbery, but this now makes me feel much better. Living in Mariposa where Stephen Leacock summered for more than twenty years, it was a real thrill to buy his story of this town. As a Leacock fan, it also gives me a good feeling to live at Southwoods, on the estate where Leacock met his wife Beatrix playing tennis on the tennis courts. Stay for a drink when you come by and we'll have a toast to Leacock."

"Will do," said Greg. "A great idea."

Chapter 29

Taking a break from his desk, Clancy was watching traffic on the street outside the office and the comings and goings of shoppers and strollers. Then he recognized, coming along the street, Pops, more formally known as Mr. Dithers who had decided to pay him another irritating visit.

"What can I do for you?" said Clancy, banging his baton on the desk so hard that it made a loud clatter. The noise of a baton can be very intimidating, and he wanted to scare Mr. Dithers off.

"You're just the man I want to see about the disgraceful behavior going on in Centennial Park, opposite the lake, right now."

"Let me guess. fornication is going on under the Hudson Bay blankets during a church picnic?"

"No. I will start at the beginning. This morning I was reading my novel, *Sense and Sensibility* by Jane Austen, under a tree in the park, catching the cool breezes blowing off Lake Couchiching. It was very quiet on the lake, no motorboats roaring about, just calm and restful. Then, down the road marched a group of young women in tight shorts and flip flops, chanting and shouting, holding placards over their heads. *'Free the Breasts. Free women, against Re-straints. Throw off your shackles'.*

"They were shouting that *women should have equal rights. Men bare their chests. Women should have the right to bare their breasts. What law says we can't?* They stopped in front of that Samuel de Champlain monument erected in 1925. The great explorer is standing on a plinth, his cloak unfurled, above a fur trader and missionary with a colonial depiction of indigenous people sitting at their feet. It's an historic monument set up to mark

Champlain's landing in 1613. He spent the winter here with the indigenous people.

"There's no place for such ribaldry in this historic setting. On a prearranged signal, the group standing in a circle, tore off their T-shirts right in front of me, showing off their jiggling breasts. I couldn't believe my eyes. I thought I would go blind. These young women showed no shame at all.

"I closed my book with a bang, got up and went over to the nearest demonstrator and said. 'Miss, cover yourself up. Have you no thought of decency in a public place?'

"She said, 'what's it to you, Pops?' She shoved her bare tits against my chest. I almost had heart failure and felt faint with this young woman assaulting me with her two big melons."

Clancy fought hard to suppress a smile.

"What are you going to do about it? This is public nudity in a public park, where children and parents come to enjoy the outdoors, to enjoy family life."

Clancy thought for a moment. "They're not still there, are they, Pops?"

"No, I don't think so. In the time I got up here to get you to come, they may have scattered."

"They need a parade permit to demonstrate like that. It may have been the heat of the day that set them off. Like that expression *mad dogs and Englishmen go out in the noon day sun*. It may have affected their thinking, a temporary lapse," suggested Clancy

"I don't think so. It was a political manifesto."

"If they come in here, naked, throwing their bare knockers around, I'll give them a good whack with my baton. I will arrest them. That's the best I can do for you."

"What has society come to?" moaned Mr. Dithers, "when a man can't quietly read his book in a park on a sunny day."

"The young are restless," admitted Clancy. "Everyone is young once. Good day, Mr. Dithers."

A very frustrated old man left the office, muttering thunder and damnation, under his breath.

Chapter 30

Clancy took a deep breath, closed his eyes and rubbed his temples. He needed a cup of coffee to inspire him. He got up, walked over and picked up the glass coffee carafe sitting on a burner. He poured himself a cup, but the light had been switched off. Cold coffee. He spat it out. Greg really must get a handle on this. He would send out for fresh coffee, but no one was in the room. With a sigh of irritation, he went back to his desk. The smell of apple cores and banana skins hit him from the waste bin, another thing for Greg to take care of.

Clancy pulled at his desk drawer to get a fresh pad of paper. He gave it a hard yank. The whole drawer came out on the floor. "Damn!"

He drew a line on the paper. Under it he wrote the name, Harold Steppes. Harold Steppes was the third man on the list who was threatening Reg Law. The other two weren't very promising suspects because of their age. Where can I find him? He'd received a manslaughter sentence, of ten years eligible for parole after serving three years, with time off for good behavior, and put on probation for the rest of his life. But this judgment was overturned, and he was released. Forensic evidence later proved that his wife had accidentally slipped and fallen down the cellar stairs, hitting her head on the bottom step, giving her a hematoma on the brain. It burst, bleeding out in the brain, followed by death. The crown apologized to Steppes for his unjust conviction.

Clancy contacted the parole board for the last address and phone number of Harold Steppes. He phoned the number. An old lady answered the phone in a quivering voice. "Harold Steppes, no such person lives here." The next Steppes he found in the Barrie listing, and he tried that. A recorded message said, *this phone is no longer in service.*

Clancy thought that Steppes would have had to keep in contact with the parole board and had to provide a permanent address for them. Somebody at the parole board had slipped up. His cross Canada search revealed two Steppes in Mariposa. To the first number listed on the third ring, a young male voice answered.

"Harold Steppes?"

"You must want my uncle. He lives in the country, in Coldwater, Ontario, just north of here."

"Do you happen to have his phone number?"

"Hold on. I'll see if I find get it. "Clancy could hear the TV blaring in the background. "Maude, have you seen my address book?"

He came back on the line. "Here it is. RR1. Coldwater, Ontario. Tel 705-555-5555."

Clancy thanked him. Coldwater was a small hamlet, of 12,000, north of Mariposa. Highway 12 runs through the middle of the village. It's near the crime scene at Port Severn, thought Clancy. Instead of phoning, I'm going to drive up, look around and have a little chat. There's just one main street and several smaller side streets. His place wouldn't be too hard to locate.

It only took about 20 minutes to reach Coldwater, a pretty village surrounded by trees and green fields, with a mixture of old Victorian houses and modern one level ranch style homes.

The Coldwater Post Office, several churches, the post office and a scenic mill on the river just about summed it up. On the outskirts of the village, he found what he was looking for. He knocked on the door of a dilapidated building that could only be described as a shack.

Used bicycle and car tires were littered the front lawn, with parts from a car battery, an engine, tires and old car seats scattered near the house. A battered truck was in the driveway. In the shed by the shack was parked an expensive Harley Davidson motorcycle.

Clancy walked up to the screen door which had several holes in the mesh for flies to get in. He knocked several times, then banged louder when no one answered. He must be in, there's his truck. thought Clancy.

A tall, muscular man, in jeans and leather jerkin, wearing a ponytail, appeared at the door. "Yeh, what do you want?"

"Harold Steppes?"

"Yeh, that's me. What do you want?"

"I'm here to ask you a few questions. Do you mind if I come in?" Clancy flashed his ID.

"It's perfectly fine by me to answer them standing right here."

"Do you know the name, Reg Law?" asked Clancy

Steppes scratched his head, "No."

"I will refresh your memory. He's the one you threatened the day you were sentenced for manslaughter. He acted as crown in your case."

"Did he? It's a long time ago and my memory is not good."

"Less than seven years ago."

"So what?" asked Steppes belligerently.

"It appears that he's been murdered. Drowned, up at the locks, with a big suspicious bump on the back of his head. Where were you five nights ago, and can anyone vouch for you?"

"See here, are you insinuating I had something to do with this? Plenty of people make threats but don't carry them out. For your information, I was walking the dog then drove down to Mariposa and sat down for a pint at the pub Brewery Bay."

"O.K. "said Clancy," did you talk to anyone in the pub that night?"

"Of course, several people."

"Give me a name and I'll check it out for the purpose of elimination."

"Tony Gibbs."

Clancy wrote it down. "I'll see what he has to say. Stick around Harry. Don't go too far. We'll need to talk again."

"I've done my time, this is nothing but harassment. The police try to stick it to you when they have no other suspects, no evidence and no proof. They like to go fishing."

"Be that as it may," said Clancy, closing his notebook. Harry looks the most promising suspect so far besides the boyfriend, he thought.

Chapter 31

The one place Harold Steppes mentioned where he liked to drink was Brewery Bay in Mariposa with Tony Gibbs, his alibi for the night the murders were committed. Clancy looked at his watch, going on 4.30, nearly time for Happy Hour. So, he headed back down the highway to Mariposa and the Brewery Bay. Several couples were standing at the bar, including two businessmen talking about the stock market. He went up to the bar and asked the bar tender, "Do you know a guy by the name of Tony Gibbs?"

"It's a bit early for him. But I saw him sitting over there by the wall, talking to someone. Yeh, just a short time ago. He's probably there now."

Clancy wandered over to the occupied table. The two men stopped speaking. "You Tony Gibbs?" One of the men turned towards him, a tall, skinny young man in jeans and sneakers.

"Harry Steppes gave me your name. He said you were with him several nights ago here at the pub."

"Yeh, for what's it's worth. I'm here most nights for a pint. Like to meet my friends, keep up with what's going on. What's this about?"

"He needed an alibi and you were it."

"Yeh, I can vouch for him. I don't see him here every night. sometimes he goes up to the Roundhouse for a drink.

"He does, does he?"

"Yeh, that place out of town that has a band some nights and where there's dancing. "

The Roundhouse. That place rang a bell with Clancy. Wasn't that where Mira had had her run in with some jerk on a motorcycle?

Harold has a motorcycle. Could it be the same person? It's a long shot. Don't go jumping to conclusions he cautioned himself.

Leaning closer, Clancy asked, "Tony, what do you work at? Can I contact your employer for a reference?"

"Oh, pleeeze, none of that fancy stuff. I'm on unemployment insurance, got laid off like half the country."

"Where can I contact you if you're not here?"

"I live here in Mariposa in a rooming house on Brant Street. I've got nothing to hide."

"What's the address? The owner's name? I will have to check it out, for the purpose of elimination."

"Be a nice guy. Don't try to ruin my chances of living here, huh?"

"Don't worry. I'll be discreet."

Yeh, thought Tony, like a bull in a china shop.

Chapter 32

As soon as he got out of the bar Clancy got hold of Greg on his phone and told him to check out the landlord of the rooming house where Tony Gibbs lived.

"Will do." said Greg. "I'll call now." He punched in the number.

"Is Mr. Henry there?" asked Greg.

"Do you want to rent a room?" asked the person who answered. "No? I'm a renter myself. But I can tell you we're full up. Hold on, I'll get him."

Greg identified himself. "Mr. Henry, I'm making inquiries about one of your tenants, Tony Gibbs."

"What's he done?"

"Nothing. I just wanted to find out if he's behind in his rent or have you had any other problems. How reliable is he?"

"Fine so far. He's secretive, keeps to himself, minds his own business and is not a problem as far as I can see. Will that do?"

"Yes, "thanks said Greg and rung off.

That trail had gotten a little colder, but not to worry.

***

Clancy headed over to the law offices of Law and Stone, he wanted to talk again to Mel Stone, to get some further help, further insight, feedback into the murder investigation. Two heads were better than one. He walked in and found efficient Miss Neat on her computer happily typing away. "I wish to speak to Mel Stone."

"I'll ring through and see if he's free. He may have a client with him at the moment, which means you'll have to wait."

Clancy waited.

Miss Neat buzzed Mel Stone when the client came down the hall to leave.

"Okay, you can go through now."

Clancy walked along the hall to Mel Stone's office. "Thanks for seeing me at such short notice."

"How is your murder investigation going?"

"Not well. If I concentrate on who killed Reg Law, then I have the three names that you gave me, the three men who threatened Reg. Two are too old and don't have the strength or the motivation. One man is dead, run over by a cyclist the other day and had a heart attack. The other one is elderly and strikes me as a recluse."

"Don't be fooled by their age," said Mel. "Age doesn't stop them. So? What about the third one?"

"The only other suspect so far lives up in Coldwater near the locks. He would be well acquainted with the area and the crime scene."

"That sounds like a good bet."

"Yeh, I should go and have another chat with him. But, on the other hand, the murderer might have been planning on just killing Debbie Love, and Reg Law just happened to be in the way. In this case the prime suspect would be her boyfriend. So, for now I have to find a connecting thread in all of these suspects.

'The interesting thing is that Debbie Love was taken by Reg Law to dinner at the Riverhouse Restaurant up in Port Severn the evening she was murdered. The waitress identified her and that she had been there several times on dates with Reg Law."

"Does that surprise you?"

"No, it doesn't. Strange things can happen, human nature being what it is."

"You've got your work cut out for you."

"So has my partner, Greg, who's working on the break-in at Judge Wiffy's, all the things that were stolen. The manuscript for Sunshine Sketches has just turned up."

"That's good to hear."

"If you think of anything, just give me a shout," said Clancy heading out.

Chapter 33

Greg had decided to do some more sleuthing, to try to locate some of the items from Judge Wiffy's robbery. In a small town like Mariposa, the next best place to the pawn shop to look was the bars where the stuff could be quickly unloaded for fast cash, no questions asked.

His first stop was the Legion hall down by the lake. He wasn't a member, but the public was welcomed to come in and have a drink. He parked his car in the parking lot and walked in.

Several solitary veterans were sitting in the sunlit room by the glass plate window bending a few, looking out at the harbour. Greg could see what they were looking at through the large bay window.

It was a beautiful afternoon. The Mariposa Belle was in her berth, with passengers walking up the gangplank to board for a tour of Lake Couchiching. Ten or more yachts were moored along the floating docks jutting out onto the lake. Men looked up at him with rheumy eyes. Greg thought no, not a good bet to question them. They wouldn't have the extra cash to buy purloined goods on their old age pensions. If they did have extra cash it would go towards a pint.

But the young guy at the next table could. Greg walked over to the man hunched over a drink.

"Anybody try to sell you stuff lately in here?"

"Yes, fancy you should ask that, a guy came in yesterday afternoon about this time, saying he wanted to unload some stuff found in his parents' attic."

Greg's ears perked up at the words 'parents' attic'. "Continue."

"He had some hockey memorabilia, some coins and a watch."

"Can you describe him to me?"

"Tall, slim, dark haired, dressed in jeans, scruffy type, wearing sneakers."

"Any distinguishable marks on his face or his hands?"

"Not that I noticed. Oh yes, he had a small dragon on the back of his hand."

"Any idea where he lived or can be found? Did he give a name?"

"Nah, he just wanted to make a quick sale. I think he said the name, Tony. It could be a fake name. My guts told me that the stuff was hot. I didn't believe a word he said."

"Thanks for your time."

The description matched Tony Gibbs. Could this be same the guy Harold Steppes gave Clancy as his alibi? Time to find out.

On his way back up the street from the Legion he passed the LCBO outlet. He recognized the bum pissing against the wall, an old familiar face, Freddie, the alky. He was known to linger on street benches and alleyways in and around Mariposa and then dossing down in Centennial Park to sleep, day or night.

Yellow. rheumy eyes, greased black hair, thin cheeks, missing front teeth; kicked in, probably during a fight. A thin and wasted figure, his pants torn at the knees, no socks, holes in his shoes, red plaid shirt, probably donated by the Salvation Army. There was a dark, wet urine stain on the fly of his pants.

He had been arrested several times for loitering and being a nuisance. Greg decided to bring him.

"Get in, Freddy we're going for a short ride. "

Freddie hung his head and docilely got in. Greg hoped that he'd not vomit or piss on the back seat.

As they entered the office, Clancy got up from his desk. "What is it this time?".

"Guess who we found pissing on the wall at the LCBO. Our friend, Freddie the alky, in full view of the public."

"Why did you do that in public, Freddie? Why not an alley or behind some bushes where no one can see you?" Clancy shook his head.

"When you gotta go, you gotta go," mumbled Freddie.

"What have we here?" He glanced down at Freddie's

arthritic hands, all knobs and bones. On his little finger was a shiny gold signet ring. "Now, where did you get that? Did you steal it?" Clancy looked more closely. It had the scales of justice engraved on it.

"A little too rich for you. Where did you get it?" he thundered, smashing his baton down on the desk.

Freddie jerked his hand away. "I just got it. I paid for it fair and square."

"Where from?" demanded Clancy

"This guy comes along, a peddler outside the LCBO. he opened his wind breaker and showed me a few things."

"A peddler? Tell me another one. There are no peddlers around here, only thieves getting rid of their stuff."

"I believed him. Anyhow he showed me this ring."

"How did you pay for it? You've got no money. It all goes on drink."

"I used the money I'd collected returning bottles, beer cans, and hand outs to pay for it. He'd seen me around. He offered me a deal that I couldn't refuse."

"What did he look like?"

"Tall skinny guy in jeans, long black hair."

"Did he have a dragon tattoo on the back of his hand?"

"I wasn't paying that much attention. My eyes aren't good."

Clancy grabbed him by his shirt collar. "The ring is stolen, Freddie. You've harboured stolen goods. I have to believe your story, though I don't want to. I'm taking the ring. It belongs to Judge Wiffy." He grabbed Freddie's finger and wrenched it off.

"Ow, that hurts. You can't do that. I got it fair and square."

"Oh yes I can. We might drop the charges of public nudity for pissing in public, Freddie. We might look the other way. It's up to you."

Freddie gave Clancy a dirty look and shrugged his shoulders. Greg led him to the door. "Don't let me catch you again." He closed the door behind Freddie. "He needs a good boot in the behind. Judge Wiffy will be glad to get the ring back."

***

The water cooler in the office needed filling. So humid and hot although Clancy was not keen on drinking water. He looked around the office. Sunshine was pouring through the dust coated windows. Below them, the air conditioner wheezed away. They needed blinds. There were a lot of things they needed, but the police budget wasn't big enough. However, he was glad he wasn't living out on the prairies where wildfires were burning continuously.

The phone rang. It was Judge Wiffy. "How's the investigation coming along? I was glad to get the ring back. Any further news?"

"We're pursuing several lines of inquiry," said Clancy. "We have to be patient. It takes time."

"Be sure to let me know of any developments."

"Will do."

One thing for sure, they had to keep Judge Wiffy happy, an important contact at the courthouse was always useful.

***

What to pursue next? Clancy decided he needed more background on Debbie Love's private life. There were a lot of blank spaces to fill in. Who would know? Debbie Love's roommate, Patty Blake.

"Hey David, another interview with Patty Blake is needed. You have a lot of charm with the ladies."

"Are you being sarcastic?" asked David.

"Nooooo," said Clancy but he grinned just the same.

David got into his car and drove over to the house, hoping on the off chance to catch Patty after her yoga class at the Y. Instead of waiting in his hot car for her, he decided the wicker chair on the veranda was a more comfortable place to sit in while catching the cooling breezes blowing off the lake. He rang her bell but there was no answer.

A fat-cheeked chipmunk scurried across the lawn and dived into a hole under the veranda. A grey squirrel that had been digging in the ground, lifted its head and stared at him then commenced digging again. Several black crows perched on the overhead wire looked down. In the tall grass, a grasshopper leaped up. Summer was finally here.

David didn't have to wait long. Patty, in a long ponytail, with her blue yoga mat swung across her shoulders in a sling, wearing her black, lululemon yoga pants, pink T-shirt and sneakers, strode up the walk. She looked hot and tired. She seemed surprised to see him sitting there quietly waiting for her.

"Hi, Patty, I just dropped by to ask you a few more questions. I won't take much of your time," said David.

Patty pulled up another chair and sat down beside him. Then she took off her bandana to wipe the sweat off her forehead. "I'd like to offer you a cool glass of lemonade, but I haven't shopped for groceries this week yet."

"I'm okay, thank you. Rest your feet. Can you fill me in on some background on Debbie? Can you tell me more about who Debbie went out with besides her boyfriend, Gary Potts? You told me that she had started seeing another man besides Gary in the last little while, someone you suspected was married. Someone she was very secretive about. Can you describe him to me? Can you recall any details? How tall he was? Fat or thin? Balding? Middle aged or younger?"

"I never got a good look at him. He never came upstairs. He always sat in the car's driver's seat in the driveway which was kind of strange. Not friendly like. Patty made no effort to introduce me to him."

"Here is Reg Law's picture. Does that look like him?"

"It kind of looks like him, but I'm not sure." Patty shook her head. "He was an older guy. But I didn't get a good look at him."

"What kind of car did he drive?"

'A black Chev."

David nodded, that was Reg Law's car.

"I remember another time, he came by in a black SUV."

"A different car?" said David, pricking up his ears. "That's interesting."

"Yes," nodded Patty.

"Do you think that he was the same driver and had just used another car?"

"I don't know." said Patty shaking her head.

David thought this was a new development. It opened up the possibility that different cars meant different drivers came to pick up Debbie which could mean that Debbie was going out with two different men.

Just then they were interrupted as a tall man in his early thirties, with long blonde hair wearing Bermuda shorts, T-shirt and sandals came up the walk.

"Hi, Patty. Sorry to interrupt. Dropped by to see how you're doing."

"Hi, Bill." In an aside to David, Patty said, "Bill Storm is one of my friends from the Y. Occasionally he bumped into Debbie down at Brewery Bay. David Scott of the OPP is asking about Debbie's lifestyle and her social contacts, Bill. Can you help us out?"

"I can try," said Bill.

"Bill, can you tell me a little about her social life down at Brewery Bay, people she talked to?"

"Well, in the beginning, I fancied her myself. But she didn't give me the time of day. She blew me off. She liked the older guys, the Sugar Daddies, who were loaded from what I could see. They were always chatting her up and vice versa."

"Did you ever see her leave with anyone?"

"I wasn't watching her that closely."

"So, you saw no specific person talking to her? Or the same person talking to her over a period of time?"

"That's right. No one stood out."

"Thanks for your help."

Bill sat down beside Patty and put his hand affectionately on her knee. "Hope things are getting better."

"Yes, slowly. Thank you. That's nice of you to ask."

"Getting back to my line of questioning, Patty. How often did you see the black SUV?" asked David.

"Several times."

"You never saw the driver or got a good look at him?"

"No. He never came in. I really wasn't paying attention. It's hard to get a good view from the upstairs window. He would just honk his horn to let her know that he was there.

"She would look out the window, wave and then go down to meet him. He never got out of the car to open the door for her. So, I can't tell you much."

Behind them they heard a fierce banging on the living room window. A stooped old lady with grey hair shook her fist at them, "Too much noise," she shouted, "too much noise. Clear off, or I'll call the cops."

"That crazy old bat. Ignore her," said Patty. "I have as much right to sit out here on the verandah as she does."

David figured it was time to go.

"Well, thanks for your help, Patty. Any information is valuable in a murder case. We're trying to put together the pieces of the puzzle, to build up a picture of what Debbie was like. If you think of anything else, please get in touch. Here's my card." He gave one to Patty and one to Bill Storm.

Chapter 34

When David got back to the office, he shared his information with Clancy. A black SUV, that doesn't give me much to go on, mused Clancy a license number would be more helpful. This would be like finding a needle in a haystack. But I can make inquiries around. Maybe I didn't ask Tim Holt, the right questions or enough questions. I need to interview him again.

It was time to take another spin up to Port Severn to talk to Tim Holt.

It was a nice afternoon for a drive, the sun was coming out, the lake was a sparkling blue and, as he drove through the wetlands in north Mariposa, he saw the osprey flying overhead.

Clancy noticed the highway sign, 'Beware Bears', near a blueberry patch and then. later, up the road, 'Deer Crossing.' He slowed down. There had been some nasty collisions involving deer.

At Port Severn locks he found the park and next to it, Tim, wearing a green T- shirt and jeans was at his usual spot with his pole and tackle, fishing. A few seagulls flew overhead. A bald-headed eagle sat perched high in a tree waiting for its next catch.

"Can I have a word, Tim?"

Tim reeled in his line and carefully put down his pole, then turned to Clancy.

"Have you caught anything yet?" asked Clancy.

"Just one medium sized perch and a large trout." Tim gestured at his fishing basket. Clancy looked down at the fish wrapped in old newspaper.

"Not bad. Tasty when fried with butter. Tim, I wanted to ask you if you recall seeing a car parked near here, several nights ago. It would have been parked here for about two to three hours. It was a black Chev, a fairly new model, 2016. You may have passed it on your way home after fishing. There were two people in the car, a middle- aged man and a young woman. Did you see a car like I'm describing?"

"No, I don't recall seeing it parked here."

"Did you see anyone else around here? Another car? Another person on foot? Have you seen any peeping Toms or guys hiding in the bushes? Or single men playing with themselves in the front seat of their cars parked in the parking lot? Or some guy sitting alone on a bench watching the scenery day after day? Vagrants? Homeless men?"

"No. Not really. Nothing like that. There's one old guy, kind of creepy, who likes to come by and talk to anyone who is fishing, asking questions about what they've caught etc. But he's harmless. He's the only one who hangs around here. Cars come and go on the highway. Some pause for a short time, while the passengers take in the view. But no one hangs around the parking lot for a long time."

Clancy was putting away his notebook, when Tim stopped him and said, " Now that you ask as I left the area I was heading home and it was getting dark I did see a black SUV pull into the parking lot shortly afterwards, around 8.30 p.m. "

"Did you get the license plate number? Can you remember what the driver looked like?"

"No, I wasn't paying too much attention. All I wanted to do was get home and clean my fish and put them into the freezer."

"Did you notice whether the driver was older or younger?"

"No, can't remember."

The black SUV again, thought Clancy. "Tim, if you can remember anything unusual, anything out of the ordinary, give me a call. Here's my card." As he got back into his car, he thought about the black SUV, very suspicious.

He felt he was getting somewhere.

Chapter 35

The weather forecast was for rain. Clancy, glancing out of the window, saw that threatening grey clouds had formed overhead. They hadn't had a lot of rain for a while, and the flowers and crops badly needed it. He heard the distant sound of thunder and a flash of lightening zapped across the sky. The office door opened, and David slouched into the office and collapsed into his chair.

"Not perky today? Not you're usually self? Were you out chasing wild women again? That can be tiring, David. That will make you old before your time. Besides that, you won't be any good on a murder investigation."

"Ah," said David. "Knock it off. Last night I just wanted a cold beer. My throat was dry. I was real thirsty. So, I figured what would be the harm in having just one beer. They can't hang you for having one beer, can they? I would slip into Brewery Bay during Happy Hour and then quickly out again. I would be faster than Jack Rabbit without any complications. So, I went in, pushed my way through the crowd and headed for the back of the bar, where it was darker. I would hide in the shadows, so I could be anonymous, so I wouldn't meet anyone, especially that young woman, Susy, the supply teacher. You know, the one I was telling you about who is out to cause me heartburn."

"Yeh, "said Clancy, licking his lips, "tell me more."

"I was slowly sipping my drink, savouring every last drop, when I heard my name being called. 'David, David.' Oh, please, please, let it not be her. But it was. Susy, the cute little blonde with the big, blue eyes, came pushing her way through the crowd. Fancy finding you in here again, she trilled, Is this your home away from home? I enjoyed meeting you, David, the other night. We had a lot of fun together. Let's do it again, sometime real soon." She pressed her breasts so far into my chest I could hardly breathe.

"I groaned and said. "Remember, Susy, there are complications, as I mentioned. Life is full of complications. Here's to us, she said as she lifted her glass up and took a big swig out of it.

"I drowned the rest of the beer in my glass as fast as I could. I had to get out of there. Trouble was brewing. Buy me one, you owe me, she said, holding out her glass. So, I bought her another one, while she giggled, and said, David, you've been a naughty boy. In the olden days, bad boys got the strap. What do they get today? Only the teacher knows, she winked up at me.

"This woman obviously is not going to take the hint," said Clancy. "You have to spell it out for her in plain English."

"Yeh, sure, and have her blab it all over the bar how he did this and that. Why do things have to get messy? Why do they have to get complicated?"

"That's the nature of the beast. Women say that men are pigs," said Clancy.

"What a pal you are when I'm in trouble."

"You have to keep saying No, nicely, until she gets the hint. It might take her a long time That's the price you have to pay for dabbling, for dipping your beak."

"That's what I thought," said David, holding his head in his hands.

"When I left, she called out to me that she hoped to see me again in the pub, real soon. I wanted to reply, 'over my dead body.'"

David retreated to his desk and sat down, opened the desk drawer, and reached for a Tylenol. Then got up to get himself a glass of water.

**

Clancy picked at his teeth with the toothpick that he got in a Chinese restaurant.

He switched on the radio.

News flash. Grisly murder scene at Port Severn Locks. Woman found bound and gagged in trunk of car. The police need your help.

Clancy flicked it off.

Whom should he focus on? Harry Steppes or the boyfriend? Both were good possibilities. Clancy decided to run it by Mel for a second opinion, the law office was close by and it was nearly time for a coffee break.

Stepping into the law office was like stepping into a meat freezer. The air conditioning was on full blast. Lois Neat, the office secretary, wearing a wool cardigan, was bent over trying to slip some legal sized files into the filing cabinet. She was shivering. Curious, she looked up at him.

"Can I get hold of Mel for a few minutes? Better still, ask him if he wants to take a break and go out for coffee at Apple Annie's."

"I'll check for you," said Miss Neat, putting down the pile of files on the desk.

She got Mel on the intercom. "Yes, he'll be out in a few minutes. Take a seat in the lounge area meantime."

He didn't have to wait long. Mel soon joined him in the lounge

"Glad that you could join me. I'll just take twenty minutes of your time. It's a short walk to Apple Annie's I want to run this by you. I need a second opinion. I'll pay for coffee."

"Anything I can do to help," said Mel "It's nice to take a break."

Clancy lined up at the counter and ordered two plain coffees, while Mel waited behind him.

Taking their coffee mugs with them, they slipped into a table near the back of the room, but they could still hear the loud voice of a woman saying, "She paid $10,000 to an agency to find a man. Money means nothing to her." "What?" her friend exclaimed, "Did she find anybody?" The conversation trailed off.

They were just about to begin talking when a big bosomed woman, a woman he didn't recognize, approached their table.

She boldly planted herself in front of him.

You're just the man I want to get hold of. I 'm Mrs. Proudfoot from the Mariposa Public Library. We're having a bake sale for Canada's Literacy Week this Saturday. All the proceeds will go towards buying new books for the library. Reading books helps keep the hoodlums off the street. I have in my hand a raffle ticket for the cakes. I hope you'll buy one. One ticket is $2.00 or three for $5.00."

"In my job, I don't have time to read," said Clancy

"Oh, that's no problem. You'll be helping others. I won't take no for an answer."

Could her voice get any louder? This woman is trying to blackmail me, in front of everyone, thought Clancy, wishing he was a thousand miles away and that Mrs. Proudfoot would step into a deep hole and disappear.

"How much are they? I guess I could buy one." He didn't want to appear a cheapskate.

She raised her voice. "Only one?"

"Mm." He reached into his trouser pocket for a toonie.

"Here's a fiver," said Mel. "I'll take three."

"Well, here they are. Thank you, gentlemen, for your participation. May you be lucky winners." She pocketed the money then walked over to the next table

Sure, thought Clancy, sure I'll win. "Thank gawd she's gone. Now I can tell you, Mel, what's on my mind."

"I'm always interested in how the case is progressing since it was my partner who was murdered," said Mel.

"Very slowly. A suspect who looks promising is Harold Steppes, who lives at Coldwater near Port Severn and is physically capable of hauling a body overland and dumping it into the lake.

"The boyfriend is another good possibility; his motive is anger or revenge. He claims he didn't know that she was going out with Reg Law and it took him by surprise when I mentioned that Debbie had dinner at the Riverhouse Restaurant an hour or so before her death.

"By the way, I hate to ask this question, but where were you on the evening of the 17th?"

"That's a strange question. Why are you asking me, of all people?"

"It's just for the purpose of elimination, nothing more. I have to ask everyone, yourself included. Just doing my job."

"I was home alone. After eating a microwave dinner, I was watching TV."

"Alone?"

"Yes, I've been divorced for several years. No alibi." He smiled confidently at Clancy.

"I'll keep in touch. If you can think of anything it would be a great help. Debbie Love's murder is sad and so hard on her parents."

Chapter 36

Clancy sent David over to interview Patty Blake again, to get a clearer picture of Debbie Love and her dating life. Her killer, he figured, must have been someone she knew or had dated. The more he found out about Debbie, the closer he felt he would get to solving the murders.

David was happy to oblige. Patty was a pretty girl, a sight for sore eyes. Too bad about the complications in his life. He could look but not touch. He drove over and parked. He spotted Patty with her eyes closed, in black yoga tights on a blue yoga mat doing the Downward Dog on the side lawn beside her house.

"Sorry to bother you again Patty, but I need your help. Can we sit down somewhere and talk?",

"Sure thing. Grab a seat on the verandah," said Patty getting up, "I'll run upstairs and bring us two cold glasses of lemonade."

David seated himself in a comfortable wicker chair with a cushion and waited for her to return.

He took a sip of the lemonade, refreshing on a hot day.

"When we last talked, Patty, you told me that Debbie was taking courses at Georgian College during the week, when she was not dating Gary Potts. and that she had no outside interests. But we have evidence to the contrary. She was leading a double life.

"Did you have any idea that Debbie was leading a double life? Did she allude to it in any way? Did she say that she was going out with someone other than the man in the black Chev? Take some time to think about it."

"None whatsoever. Debbie was secretive. We never discussed our private life. I respected her privacy." Patty shook her head. "I did notice something odd though. In the evening she dressed up to go out to classes, putting on eye make up, perfume, and wearing heels. Normally one dresses down to go to classes, wearing casual wear like jeans and a T shirt. I thought it kind of odd, but then I figured that's Debbie's style.

"Another thing I remembered just now was that she got an angry phone call a day before she went missing. I heard her shouting, 'You can't talk to me like that. How dare you call me a whore. Apologize.' I pretended that I hadn't heard her and was shocked that the word whore was even used.

"Debbie's face was flushed when she got off the phone. In front of me she seemed both angry and embarrassed by the phone call.

"Do you know who made the call here?"

"I have no idea."

"Do you think it was her boyfriend?"

Patty shook her head. "He would never talk like that to her. They never fought."

"Did she keep a day-to-day diary? Could we have a look at that? Did she have a cell phone? We could trace the calls she made or received. Or on the landline."

"No, she didn't have a cell phone. It was too expensive for her. We shared the landline." Patty brightened, "But we can look through her things that might tell us something."

Behind them, the old lady had pulled the curtain back and was staring at them. She shook her fist then shouted, "Go away. Go away."

"Let's have some privacy and go upstairs. The old lady has dementia," said Patty.

Clancy followed Patty upstairs to Debbie's room. "I'll soon have to find another roommate to help pay the rent. It's near the end of the month" sighed Patty. "Her parents are coming over tonight to take away her things."

Clancy looked around the room, at the pink coverlet on the double bed, the plumped-up pillows. A big teddy bear with a blue bow and several other stuffed animal toys, a lion, a tiger and a zebra, were sitting on the counterpane.

Across the room was her dresser, the surface crowded with cosmetics, brushes, lipsticks, powder, eyeliner, lip pencil, rouge and eye shadow. On one side were lined up her glass bottles of perfume of different colours and shapes. On the wall was a chest high portrait of Brad Pitt, a poster boy for getting fit at the gym. Tiny hooks held her necklaces, a strand of pearls and coloured glass beads. One pair of red stilettos and a pair of black patent high heels were lined up beside each other outside the closet door.

In a corner was stashed Debbie's pink backpack Patty scooped it up and threw it on the bed. She rummaged around among Debbie's notebooks and texts. "This might help." She pulled out a timetable with the dates of the week at the top of each column.

David looked at the days of the week before Debbie disappeared. For Wednesday, at the bottom, the capital letter R was written with a red ballpoint pen. That could be for Reg Law. On Thursday, at the bottom of the column, he saw a capital S, again written in red ink. Now we're onto something. S must be another man in her life. He looked for the initial again, found it for the next week and the week after, along with the letter R. He then looked at the last day in her timetable, the date that Debbie, was murdered but there were no initials. Maybe she didn't have time to put them in. Not much help. But who was S?

"Did you have a look around for Debbie's bank account book? Or do you know the bank that she banked at? Debbie's purse wasn't found at the scene of the crime."

"It must be among her things." Patty found a large shoulder bag hanging from the closet doorknob and brought it over to him.

"Check this out." She handed it to David. "It might be in here."

David scooped out the contents and laid them on the bed. lipstick, mirror, notebook, coin purse, wallet and the blue Royal Bank of Canada bank book. He picked it up and opened it.

Reading down through the entries in the deposit column, He looked for recent deposits. Every week, on a Friday, there was a deposit for $200.00.

He picked up his cell phone and phoned the bank to speak with the manager. He identified himself and mentioned the $200 amount deposited regularly in Debbie Love's chequing account. He wanted to know if this amount was paid into the account by cheque or by cash.

"Let me look for you. It will take a few minutes."

Back came the answer, "by cash". David didn't think anyone like Law, a lawyer, or S, whoever he was, would be stupid enough to pay by cheque, which would be easy to trace, but it was worth checking out. Well at least he would be looking for a man with the first or last name, with the initial, S. He thanked Patty for her help, and then went back to the office.

Chapter 37

It was a violent summer storm, beginning with black clouds overhead. Bolts of lightning zigzagged across the sky, followed by claps of thunder, then heavy rain, pelting down for five or ten minutes, then easing off, then more lightning and heavier rain. The streets were awash with water rushing toward the sewers, but the sewers were full, causing an overflow. It was weather a duck would love. Standing at the office window, Clancy was glad that he wasn't out driving in that storm. The rain coming down was so heavy one could hardly see the car ahead on the highway. Sometimes there was a gust of wind, then hail the size of bullets would pelt down.

"I bet a few trees have been zapped by the lightning and even a barn may have been hit. It's volatile weather," said David. "I'm glad I'm not out there in it. There'll be some traffic accidents no doubt."

The phone rang. It was Agnes. She sounded anxious. "We've got flooding in the basement. We'll have to get a plumber to come out after the storm is over."

This was the second time they had to get a plumber in. Expensive, thought Clancy. Why didn't he fix the problem the first time?

"Phone the neighbours, Agnes, and find out if they have the same problem. Plumbers are so expensive. He'll probably want time and a half for coming out in an emergency. Wait until I get home. It won't be long and then we'll decide what to do."

***

For David it seemed things couldn't get any worse. In his life, it never rained but it poured. Lately he was having rotten luck as far as women were concerned. At the Mariposa high school where Clara taught English, her girlfriend on the staff, another teacher named Beth Kudar who taught ESL, was getting married in August. The staff were having a shower for her, down at Brewery Bay. Clara insisted that he come along as her date because she didn't want to go alone. These parties were a woman's thing he had told her. He didn't want to stick out as the only man there. Besides, Susy was sure to be there itching to cause trouble.

He'd made up all kinds of excuses to Clara, but in the end, he caved in. Beth's fiancée and several of his colleagues were going to be there also. There would be protection in numbers. He hoped that in the crowd Susy wouldn't find him. That would be a disaster.

So, at five, 'Happy Hour,' he reluctantly joined Clara and the rest of the staff of Mariposa Collegiate down at Brewery Bay. Everyone was happy for Beth who had gone out with her high school sweetheart for several years and was now sealing the deal.

David stood back and let Clara do all the talking since she knew most of the people there. Things were going well. Toasts to the happy couple were made, a few cards and gifts were handed over to Beth who happily to received them.

Then, David recognized that little plaintive voice again, "David, so good to see you again. Where have you been hiding? I've been coming here often looking for you. I've been hoping to bump into you."

It was bright eyed Susy, in a pretty pink sun dress showing off a gorgeous tan.

Oh migawd, he thought, as he forcefully edged himself away from her, but she clung to him like Saran Wrap.

"Listen, Susy," David lowered his voice, "I can't talk now, I'm with friends and we're celebrating an upcoming wedding. Things are complicated," he hissed.

"You said that before. But here you are. Back again looking for action."

"Please keep your voice down. You're shouting."

"I have the right to speak. Don't try to hush me up. Is that your 'complication' standing next to you? She seems nice. But not as nice as me."

"Can it, will you," David glanced nervously in Clara's direction to see if she was listening.

"Ah, so your friend is maybe sensitive to what I might say," said Susy belligerently. "She would be very surprised if she found out we did the nasty, wouldn't she? It might upset your little apple cart."

"This conversation has to end now," said David. Grabbing hold of Clara's elbow, he suggested that they go over to the wall where there was more standing room. "It's too crowded here," he said.

"Sounds like a good idea," said Clara. "That little blonde is a bit pushy. trying to latch onto you like that."

"You're telling me, a little hussy," said David, with sweat dripping off his forehead, glancing behind him to make sure Susy hadn't followed them. What a close call. Things were getting ugly, but disaster had been averted.

He had learned his lesson. He wouldn't be back in here again, even on a frosty Friday.

Chapter 38

In the office, taking a long coffee break, Clancy figured that he was a long way from solving the Law/Love murder case. He sipped his coffee slowly while thinking what he should do next.

He decided it was a nice morning for a drive to Coldwater. The sun was out, the lake sparkled blue and the tiger lilies, dandelions, and purple thistles were blooming by the roadside. As he drove through the wetlands in north Mariposa, he again saw the large white and grey osprey flying overhead, flapping its great wings, probably heading to its nest.

He easily found Harry Steppes' shack, situated on the edge of the village, and pulled in. The battered Ford truck was in the driveway and the Harley Davidson motorcycle was in the shed, obvious signs that Harry was home.

He walked over to the front door and banged on it. A curtain covered a window and blocked his view so he couldn't look inside. No answer. He banged on it again. Finally, the door flew open.

"You again? What do you want this time?" snarled Harry. "I told you all I know the last time you came barging up here."

"That's a warm welcome. Thought I'd drop in and tell you, the guy that you gave as your alibi, your drinking pal, Tony Gibbs, was found drinking with Phil Short, at Brewery Bay, your hangout. The stolen goods were found in his room at his rooming house. We've got Tony Gibbs in jail on a robbery charge for break and enter. Not a good person for an alibi, Harry, not good at all. You'll have to do better than that."

Steppes shook his head. "All this is news to me. I didn't know he was a thief. Nothing to do with me."

"Sure it is. Didn't your drinking partner let slip what he was doing in his spare time, his hobby, burgling houses? While I'm up here, I thought I 'd show you a picture of Debbie Love, the girl found murdered in the trunk of a car near up at Port Severn. Is she familiar?" He held the photo in front of Steppes' face and watched his reaction.

"No, never seen her before."

"How about Brewery Bay? She hung out there after work."

"There's lots of women who hang out there. It's hard to tell one from another. Who knows?" He scratched his chin. "Yeh. Maybe I have seen her in there. So what?"

"In her timetable that she kept she wrote that she went out with S. Your last name begins with' S.'"

"There must be thousands of people with names beginning with S," said Harry heatedly, "Is this some sort of fishing expedition you're on? The police, when they have no evidence at all are always fishing, fishing to make an innocent person guilty to fit their preconceived notions of who did it and to close the book on a case. Is that all you've got, the letter 'S'? Not much to go on."

"I'm just telling you like it is. Your last name begins with 'S'. Don't go far. I want you in my sights." Clancy headed back to his car.

***

Friday night was Happy Hour, Mira in a tight, sequined, V-neck T- shirt and black leather mini skirt, squeezed her way through the throng of people laughing and chatting clustered at the bar. "Excuse me. Excuse me." The noise was tremendous.

She jostled her way past, at the same time looking for someone who she might know, someone she could stop and have a talk with, do a little market research. She didn't want to stand alone nursing a beer, feeling lonely, on a Friday night. She didn't want to feel sorry for herself because she didn't have a date. Heaven forbid. What would it do to her reputation? She paused to examine herself in the mirror above the bar. Good. Not bad. There were no red lipstick marks on her white, dentally cleaned teeth.

A male voice called out, "If it isn't our illustrious journalist, Mira, from the Mariposa Packet. I didn't think journalists drank... much."

She stopped, recognizing the voice. "Oh, it's you, Mel Stone. Looking for clients? If so, I'm not one of them." She looked him up and down appraisingly. He was a smart dresser in his open-neck shirt, expensive linen suit, Italian made leather shoes and nice gold cuff links.

"I'm not on the hustle, Mira. Like you, I drifted in for a cold one to relax at the end of the week. Can I get you one as a friendly gesture? What'll you have?"

She smiled. "Thank heavens it's not a bribe, not that I'm not open to bribery in that area. Steam Whistle would be fine."

Mel chuckled, "A pretty girl like you shouldn't be alone on a Friday night. Come, we'll find a table at the back where we can sit and chat. I'll tell the bar tender to have our beers sent there. What's new with you?"

"I'll join you, but I thought you were married. I try to keep away from married men. They're nothing but trouble," said Mira checking him out by looking down at his ring finger which was bare. There was no white band on his skin.

"You thought wrong. I'm divorced now, lonely and single, with no place to lay my head as the saying goes."

"Yeh, is it that the sob story you play on your violin to make ladies feel sorry for you? Still living in the same place?"

"Yeh, I bought out my ex wife's share." He leaned in closer, trying hard not to stare at her deep cleavage exposing her large tits. "Say," and he brushed his hand across hers, "Why don't we have a few and then head back to my place and order in supper, the Greek take-out is quite good."

"Gee, you're a fast mover. I don't go back to a man's house unless I've got to know him a bit more than saying 'hello' and 'good-bye'," said Mira pushing her chair back, trying to put some distance between them. "Besides that, It's a little too soon, Mel, it's very early in the evening. I haven't even drunk my first beer. Another thing is the two murders in Mariposa that remain unsolved that are making me a little nervous."

"Ah, Mira, you can trust me. I'll be on my best behavior, a real gentleman," cooed Mel.

"That's what they all say," said Mira, looking down at his trousers and noticing the big bulge in his groin. "I'll take a rain cheque on that if you don't mind. I just want to chill out, to relax, to celebrate the end of the week, have a couple of drinks and then go home and put my feet up."

"Your choice. You're making a big mistake," sneered Mel, "you're missing out on a good time." He grabbed his beer glass and got up abruptly from the table. "I'm going back to the bar. Don't say

I didn't invite you," he called out to her. "We could've had a real nice time together." He stomped off.

Not cool at all. What a creep. With a short fuse like that, who needs the aggravation, thought Mira. For once I made the right choice. It's better to be safe than sorry.

Chapter 39

Greg's next port of call was the Dead Tired Pool Hall, where those who lived on air, unemployment insurance, Ontario Disability and welfare hung out.

It was dingy inside. The air was stale with cigarette smoke. Old movie posters were plastered on the walls. The chairs and stools needed painting, everything needed to be freshened up. The pool tables, along with the players, were located along the back wall. Greg sidled up to the manager behind the bar, who was polishing glasses with a grey dish towel the size of a washcloth that looked filthy. The manager gave him a dirty look.

"Anyone come in lately to hock stuff?"

"We don't like that sort of thing going on in here. We're a respectably run business," said the manager stiffly, with his nose in the air.

"Yes," said one patron sitting at the bar, with his bottom of his jeans hanging out over the bar seat, "We're all on the up and up in here, most of the time. But sometimes, the odd occasion, it can happen to anybody, someone comes in short of cash, trying to sell off the family heirlooms and we try to help him out. Charity like."

Another patron who was barely awake piped up, "I agree with everything he says," then went back to laying his head down on the bar. "Just resting."

Greg repeated his question, "Seen anybody who was hocking stuff lately?" he asked the next guy on a beer stool.

"You just missed him."

"What did he look like?"

"A tall, skinny guy, in jeans and running shoes."

"What was he selling?"

"Hockey memorabilia and coins."

"Have you seen him in here before?"

"He looked familiar."

"So, he must be local?"

"Maybe. It's not for me to say. I'm no squealer."

"Thanks."

Greg knew one police informant, Jimmy Snipes, a local drug dealer. Maybe he knows where I can find Tony. Maybe Tony tried to buy drugs with his new cash. Who knows? He would put the squeeze on him.

He elbowed his way through the room until he finally found Jimmy in the back, standing by the pool table with a cue stick in his hand. "Aha, thought I'd find you here. How's your back? I thought it was injured and you're still on workmen's compensation?"

"It's coming along. What's it to you?"

"Just thought I'd drop by so that you and I could have a little friendly chat."

"Yeh?" said Snipes, wiping his nose on the back of his hand, "What's friendly about it?"

"I know that you'll help me out. You play ball. Sometimes we can look the other way." He gave Snipes a knowing look, "I'm looking for a tall, skinny guy, dark haired. The name is Tony Gibbs. Does that name ring a bell?"

Jimmy paused, chewed his lip, and then took a deep breath. "We may have crossed paths. Why are you looking for him?"

"He's peddling stolen goods again and I want to find him."

"He is, is he? Have you checked Brewery Bay? That's his usual stomping ground. He sits in the bar there in the evenings."

"Do you know who he hangs out with? Can you give me a name?"

"A guy by the name of Harry and another guy, the last name, I believe, is Short. "

"Got a first name for that?"

"Phil, try Phil."

"Thanks. We'll keep in touch."

"Don't bother. I don't need the aggravation." Snipes headed back to the pool table, taking his place in the shadows.

***

After a relaxing barbecue dinner with Agnes, Clancy set out

to weed the lawn, pulling up fat, yellow dandelions that were sprouting everywhere. It was not his idea, it was Agnes's. The leaves of these dandelions were not the fresh, tender ones that you make salads with or dandelion wine, but tough ones that had been shat on by pigeons and other birds, making them totally inedible.

He was almost finished, nearing the curb, when a small, black bushy animal with a white stripe down its centre scurried across his path. A striped kitty, aka skunk. Clancy jumped back behind his car. The skunk made a nosedive for a small space between the house foundations and the patio.

Oh, thought Clancy, this all I need, a skunk finding a home under my house. Why me? Why does it have to be me? One thing for sure, I won't tell Agnes about our uninvited guest.

Chapter 40

The next morning at the office, sitting in his swivel chair, Clancy was mulling things over. It was hard to concentrate. A fat fly was buzzing back and forth across the room, settling down every so often, then whipping itself over Clancy's head just out of reach. His chair squealed on its castors as he shifted back and forth trying to swat it. Got to get Greg to go out and buy a fly swatter from Canadian Tire and kill the damn thing, He can buy a can of Raid while he's at it.

My prime suspect is Gary Potts, he thought. Debbie's boyfriend who works out at the gym and would have no trouble at all lifting his girlfriend and stuffing her in a trunk. His motive would be jealousy. Did he get wind of the fact that Debbie was seeing someone else, Reg Law, for instance? That could cause him to snap. Did he find out where they met and killed them?

The phone rang. It was Dr. Sandy's receptionist, "Dr. Sandy wants you to come in as soon as you're able. The results from the lab report are back. Would you like to come in this afternoon?"

Clancy decided this was urgent, so he headed over to Dr. Sandy's office

In the waiting room, a fat woman on crutches got up, crunching his toe as he sat down on a chair. He suppressed a howl of pain. Then a snotty nose kid kicked a metal ball towards his shins. Thankfully, Dr. Sandy opened his door to greet him otherwise there would have been a lynching.

"I have good news," said Dr. Sandy. "We caught the mole just in time. We can freeze dry it and then excise it. It was precancerous. Benign, not malignant. I will have to get rid of it. We have to watch our skin these days, our best friend is not the sun."

Picking up a needle, he gave Clancy a quick injection at the site to anaesthetize the skin.

Clancy blanched. He hated needles. The last time he had one he had fainted.

After a few minutes, Dr. Sandy scooped out a big hollow around the mole with a knife. "There, that should do it." He picked up a band aid and carefully put it over the excised skin. "Take two Tylenol and just take it easy."

Clancy was relieved. He'd dodged another bullet. He went back to the office and twiddled his thumbs, lost in reverie over the murder cases.

Around five, Clancy decided to head over to the Y to have another chat with Gary Potts and hopefully get more answers. He parked his car and walked to the entrance. Several attractive young women in shorts, yoga tights and sneakers clattered down the stairs past him as he walked up to the second-floor weight room. They hardly gave him a second look. Fitness snobs thought Clancy.

Gary was lying on a black rubber mat doing bench push-ups and was startled to see Clancy there again. He carefully put down the barbells on the mat.

"I told you everything I know," he said, coldly.

"Well, I need some more information. Can we go downstairs to the snack bar and have a chat?"

"I hate interrupting my workout."

Clancy shrugged his shoulders. "This is a murder investigation. Do you want to talk here, or down at the station?"

"Oh, alright." Reluctantly Gary got up, wiped his hands on a white towel and followed Clancy downstairs. They sat down at a small table in the rear of the room, where it was quiet.

"My main question is, was Debbie going out exclusively with you? Were you her only lover?"

Gary's face flushed. "What are you implying? Debbie didn't run around. She was a good girl, loyal and faithful. True blue."

"Yeh," said Clancy, cynically. "You were with her on the weekends, right?"

"Yes, that's right. So?"

"What about the other nights of the week?"

"She was taking a course at Georgian College in communications. She was studying to improve herself. She was busy studying. She had no time to fool around. Stop maligning my dead girlfriend." He gave Clancy a dirty look.

"Then, how come she was found in Greg Law's car? In his trunk? The waitress up at Riverhouse Restaurant at Port Severn identified her as the dining companion of Reg Law, the married lawyer. In fact, she'd gone to dinner there several times with him."

"You must be mistaken in her identity." Gary shook his head. "Debbie wouldn't do that. Why she was found in the trunk of Reg Law's car is a mystery to me. It doesn't make sense."

"It makes sense to me. Suppose someone filled with jealousy and anger at the discovery that she was going out with someone else, raped and murdered her. As her boyfriend you're my prime suspect."

Gary swallowed hard, his Adam's apple bobbing in his throat. "Well, think again. I didn't do it," he exclaimed angrily, "You can't blame me for what happened. I loved Debbie. I want you to find the person who did this." He jabbed his finger at Clancy's chest.

"By the way, what's your mode of transportation?"

"I get around on my motorcycle."

"You're in a bad place, Gary, "You have no alibi for the time of the murders. To say that you were working out in the gym isn't good enough for me."

"So?"

"Don't wander far."

Clancy thought Gary would have to check in to the Y each time with his membership card and that would be recorded giving him a reference point. But there was no check out time recorded, he just walked through the turnstile, the beeper only went off when one of the Y's towels was being nicked.

The sky darkened overhead, Clancy hurried back to the office before the deluge hit him. The rain came pelting down. He was safely inside when a small figure, an old lady in a black plastic raincoat down to her ankles, stood in the doorway, with the door flapping back and forth in the wind. It was Miss Temple. Puddles of water dripped down to her black Oxford shoes. When she shook her raincoat, more puddles were created. She carefully unbuttoned the raincoat and let it fall. Underneath, she wore a black shawl around her thin shoulders over a black print dress which clung to her knees. She was as skinny as a rail.

Timidly she asked, "Can I come in out of the rain and sit down and rest? Otherwise I'll get soaked to my skin. I have nowhere else I can go." she gave him a woeful look. "My heart is beating fast. I have angina." She placed her frail hand on her chest.

Clancy pulled a chair over so she could sit by the window

and watch the storm outside. It was a summer storm they usually blew in quickly and left just as soon, evaporating into the warm air. How long would it last? How long would Miss Temple sit there?

"Would you like me to call you a cab, so you don't have to walk home in the rain?"

"I can't afford one.",

Drat. thought Clancy, but he couldn't use the police fund to pay for a taxi for an old lady. He could offer to pay but that would be setting a precedent. He would be inundated by old ladies dropping in, wanting him to pay for their taxi home. Nevertheless, he felt guilty not offering to pay. The old lady reminded him of his dear, departed mother on her good days. There was no reason for him to feel guilty, he reminded himself. No reason at all.

Miss Temple sat quietly peering out of the window waiting for the storm to recede. The rain soon became a trickle and then stopped. Miss Temple got to her feet, shook the water off her raincoat and put it on.

"Best of luck, Miss Temple," called out Clancy.

"Thank you. You've been so kind. "

Chapter 41

The rest of the afternoon had been warm and humid, the humidity increasing after the rainfall.

The police radio came on. *Police are no closer to solving the murders at Port Severn Locks. They are hoping witnesses will come forward. Anyone with any information...*

Clancy took the band aid off the skin on the back of his hand. The wound was healing nicely. Looking up at the clock on the far wall he saw it was now five o'clock. He decided to have a quick one down at Brewery Bay before heading home. The trouble with going home was that Agnes had always lined up chores for him as soon as he walked in the door when all he wanted to do was sit with a beer in the EZY Boy Lounge chair in the back yard and listen to the hum of bees.

After paying for his draught, he glanced around at the room looking for a familiar face. He was surprised to see at the far end sitting on a bar stool, Mel Stone. He waved. Stone acknowledged him by lifting up his beer glass.

"Mind if I join you?"

"Sure. No problem."

"Didn't think I'd find you in here," said Clancy, taking a sip of his beer. "Most lawyers work long hours."

"Like everyone else I like the odd drink at the end of the day. What's new with you? How's the investigation going?"

"Had another chat with Gary Potts, my number one suspect. He said that Debbie was a very virtuous young woman, that she didn't cheat or run around on him. When she wasn't with him, she was studying for a course she was taking at Georgian College."

"Sure, the boyfriend would say that," sneered Mel. "He was in love with her." Mel bit his lip and lowered his voice. "I hate to speak ill of the dead, but from what I heard down here at Brewery Bay, Debbie Love was an easy lay. She was a whore. She wasn't studying all the nights like she said she was. A little temptress she was. I heard she was always short of cash and needed money to pay the rent. Maybe Reg Law obliged."

"That puts a different slant on things. So, from what you're saying it could be anyone here and Reg Law just happened to be in the wrong place at the wrong time."

"Maybe." Mel shrugged his shoulders. "I just heard that she wasn't Snow White. She reminded me of my ex-wife, all innocence on the surface, but a hot bitch on the inside. She was hot to trot. My ex-wife took me to the cleaners financially in the divorce settlement, even though she was the one running around. Sex and cash were her game," he said, bitterly.

"The more I interview the suspects, the more the trail narrows," said Clancy. "Harold Steppes lives in the vicinity and he was in jail for a short period of time, then let out for a miscarriage of justice. The dots are more difficult to connect in his case. Whereas, with Gary Potts, the boyfriend, if he had suspected that she was running around, he might have turned violent. But, at this point in time, I have no evidence to prove it."

"Well keep digging in that direction. Rome wasn't built in a day."

"It's a hard slog, so few clues." Clancy finished his beer. "One beer is enough for me. Got to go home and do yard work, pull up the weeds, cut the grass, that sort of thing. How about you?"

"Oh, I'll go home, pop a dinner in the microwave, watch the Blue Jays on TV. Nothing too exciting."

Chapter 42

Where to find Tony Gibbs? Greg decided to act on a hunch, it wouldn't hurt to have a look at Tony Gibbs' room in the rooming house on Coldwater Street. He didn't have a warrant to search which meant that he had to convince a judge that there were stolen goods hidden inside. He didn't have enough evidence at this point in time, but maybe he could suggest a few creative approaches to the owner, Mr. Henry.

He drove over to the house and looked at all the mailboxes lined up on the wall outside the front door. He buzzed and Mr. Henry came up the stairs from the basement, where he'd been busy replacing a burnt-out fuse. He was wheezing and panting. "Someone put on the toaster and the coffee maker at the same time. You'd think they'd know better."

"I want to have a look around Tony Gibbs' room."

"Do you have a search warrant?"

"No."

"No?"

"But you can go in and check for a radiator leaking, a tap running, a thermostat on higher than it should be. Think of something," suggested Greg.

"Usually, according to the landlord tenants act you have to give twenty-four hours notice, unless it's an emergency."

Greg gave him a withering look, "Say it was an emergency."

"Oh, alright." Mr. Henry fumbled in his trouser pocket. He slowly took out his keys, found the right one and inserted it in the lock on Tony Gibbs' door.

"There you go."

"Stand by the door and keep an eye out. I don't want to be interrupted," said Greg.

Greg was nervous about what he was going to do. He had no search warrant and what if Tony Gibbs came back suddenly, armed with a knife or a gun?

He took a look around the room. It was a plain room with a single, unmade bed, a desk that held only a small notebook, a bookshelf with several thriller paperbacks by Clive Cussler, a dresser bureau with underwear spilling out of it and a closet. Not much to see. A cockroach ran across the floor to a crack in the floorboards. A fishing rod was leaning against the wall. Above it hung a blue and white Blue Jay's pennant.

On the windowsill lay an opened Pizza Pizza box with a couple of withered crusts. Empty beer cans were lined up along the ledge. Greg ran his hand along the top of the desk, dust. He pulled open the desk drawer, and found a tube of Colgate, a toothbrush, and nail clippers. Then in the left-hand drawer he found masking tape, a yellow cigarette lighter, a screwdriver, a hammer, pliers, bolt cutters and a wrench. Tools of the burglary trade. Then he ran his hand behind a stack of paperbacks, nothing.

Next, he approached the dresser and felt in amongst the tumbled T-shirts, underwear and socks, again nothing. He then headed for the closet and opened the door. A big beige moth flew out over his head.

Greg's ears perked up at the sound of floorboards creaking along the hall. The sound of footsteps came up to the door. Greg held his breath and waited. Then the footsteps receded.

A large pine box with a sturdy lock was on the top shelf. It was heavy. He brought it down and placed it on the bed. Then he reached into his pocket for his set of master keys. One fitted. The lock popped open.

"Ho, ho, what have we got here! Looks like we've hit pay dirt," said Greg, recognizing some of the items from Judge Wiffy's robbery. A stash of paraphernalia, probably from several robberies, was inside. He opened the door and spoke to Mr. Henry who was still standing guard outside.

"Put a padlock on the outside of the door so he can't get back in, I'll get someone to come and make a complete inventory of these stolen items. If you see him, phone 911 immediately. He might show up back here or he may have gotten wind of our looking for him and done a runner. Got that?"

"Yes, "said Mr. Henry. "He's not getting back in here. I won't have a thief living here."

Greg walked back to his car. Now, where could he find Tony Gibbs?

But first he would check in at the office.

Chapter 43

I'm just a glorified gofer in that office, low man on the totem pole thought Greg.as he stood in line at Apple Annie's with Clancy and David's order.

He glanced around the room, at the mothers with young children in strollers, the seniors out for a morning break, the businesspeople wanting their jolt of caffeine. At a far table, he spotted Mel Stone, in a close face to face chat with stylishly dressed Mrs. Law, who appeared to have quickly recovered from her bereavement. Now, he thought, isn't that interesting, I'll have to tell Clancy that those two are cozy. Wonder what they're talking about?

Greg got the coffee and took it back to the office. "I've got important things to do," he said to Clancy.

He headed over to Brewery Bay, searching once again for Tony Gibbs. He hoped he would find him here this time. Greg had been returning to this place so often in the last few days that the management must think he was an alcoholic.

"Back again," said the bar tender. "Your home away from home. You're in luck. They just came in. Tony Gibbs and Phil Short that skinny guy in jeans and cowboy boots, are over there, knocking back a few."

Greg looked over at the table. Tony's eyes flashed in recognition, then he abruptly jumped up, pushed away the table and made a run for it, pushing and shoving people aside, knocking over tables, splashing beer on jackets, in his desperate attempt to reach the door and get away.

"Stop thief," yelled Greg. "Stop thief. Don't let him get away." Greg crashed after him, as fellow drinkers moved aside. But

Tony kept on going.

Just as he got to the door, the bouncer, a big burly guy with a barrel chest finally came to life, blocking the way like a football player.

"Help me," Greg cried out. "Someone help me." He reached out and grabbed Gibbs' collar and spun him around, then threw him to the ground. "Someone call 911. I need," he yelled.

Greg knelt on Tony's back then sat down on top of him.

"Get off me," shouted Tony, "I haven't done anything wrong."

"My friend is innocent. What's he done? This is police brutality," yelled Phil Short, coming to aid his fallen friend.

"Your friend's a break and enter artist. We've found stolen goods in his rooming house. Now, Tony, save your yelling for the judge. He'd like to hear what you have to say."

They didn't have to wait long. With a pugilistic air Clancy strode in the door, twirling his baton, heading straight over to them. "Lie still or I'll give you a crack on back of your head. Tony Gibbs, we've been looking for you for some time. I'll read you your rights and then we're off to the pokey. I've got a nice warm cell set aside for you. Come away quietly or you'll get whacked."

"I'm innocent. I'm innocent."

"Sure you are. Every convict in Kingston Pen says they're innocent, but the judges thought differently. Judge Wiffy is one of the people you stole from and he'll be pleased to get some of his stuff back. Come along now. You can pray that he's not one of the judges that you will have to go before." He frog-marched Gibbs out of the door, with his hands in handcuffs behind his back.

***

Meanwhile, on Mississauga Street, after walking quickly past the Sock Drawer store, Horace Dithers figured he didn't need a pair of extra socks and, at Perfect Timing Shop, his watch didn't need winding. Horace Dithers stood in front of the large window of the Bird House shop. He looked at birdbaths. That meant getting out the hose and filling them with water every day, and the bird seed feeders, which meant greasing the pole to keep the squirrels from climbing up. He decided that a bird house hanging in a tree would be easier and called for less maintenance. Maybe he should buy one for the robins in his garden to nest in. Perhaps outside his kitchen window? Should he get a large one with two perches or a small one with one perch?

Another pair of blue eyes met his reflection in the window. He whirled around and stared at her. Aha, he recognized her, the brazen young woman in shorts and top from the *Baring the Breast* protest the other day in Centennial Park, in front of the historic Champlain monument.

"Hey, Pops, what's up with you?"

"My name is Horace Dithers, I'll have you know."

"No offense. Weren't you the old guy sitting in the park reading your book when we were on that march the other day? You got very excited, jumping up and down, shouting." She rolled her eyes. "You don't want to get prosecuted for sexual assault at your age. You're too old to go to jail."

"Excited? Angry is more the correct word, at the public display of nudity put on by you young women. Miss, what is your name? I assume you're not married. No married woman would strip in public."

"My marital status has nothing to do with it. Women want equal rights, married or single. I'm a nursing mother who is legally allowed to nurse in public." She pulled out a voluminous breast and shoved it at him. "See, you don't get ones the size of these unless you're nursing a little one. "

Dithers blanched, then stepped back, his heart palpitating wildly. He was going to have a heart attack. Here on the main street this woman was exposing herself. Outrageous! Where were the police when you needed them?

"Madam, I don't see any baby here," said Mr. Dithers, stiffly backing away from her and trying to put as much distance between them as possible. He squeaked, "You should cover yourself up for decency's sake. This is a public sidewalk. People will stare. You could get arrested for indecent exposure."

"My little one is over there in the shade, in a stroller, while I shop. I'm only doing what mother nature intended for me to do, feed my cub. Let the public stare, it's good for them."

"It sounds to me like child abandonment," said Dithers.

"My baby is never out of my sight. You're the one who should be locked up, interfering with people's rights."

With this brassy, bold woman who had absolutely no shame, Dithers knew he would get nowhere, so he backed away and hurriedly headed down the street for a nice calming cup of chamomile tea. He needed something to settle his nerves. What was this next generation coming to? Not much.

There was no use going into the police station to mention this infraction. That police officer, Clancy, was useless.

Chapter 44

David dropped his black backpack in the corner of the office and sighed. "Tuesdays always get me down after a long weekend."

"Been away for the long weekend?" asked Clancy.

"Went with Clara to the Mariposa Folk Festival, in Tudhope Memorial Park. It was incredibly hot, but the breeze off Lake Couchiching kept the heat at bay. It was so relaxing sitting under the shade of the big trees, listening to folk bands on the various stages spread out through the park. We took lawn chairs and a blanket, brought a picnic, and ate our lunch there.

"The music was great, various acts and instruments, like the fiddle, the violin, the accordion, drums, very casual. Gordon Lightfoot was the headliner Sunday evening. He closed the show. He originally came from Mariposa, did you know that? Sang in St. Paul's United Church choir."

"Who doesn't?"

"Well I was lining up for a beer at the beer tent when I got into conversation with this guy who said he and his girlfriend had spent the two nights in a pup tent, along with other campers in a security controlled area on the park grounds. They couldn't afford a hotel. They had a hard time sleeping. You can't roll over in a pup tent. Anyhow, he said he would never do it again, the noise during the night was tremendous. They never slept a wink."

"Noises in the night, huh?" Clancy chuckled. "Those noises in the night are something else. Well David, my boy, forget about the noises, we have two murders to solve and I need your input.

He pulled a sheet of paper off his scratch pad and took a pen from the desk.

"Here's what we've got. Patty, her roommate, showed me Debbie Love's timetable with a capital 'S' scrawled at the bottom for several of her evenings. Who is 'S'? She also said another car besides Reg Law's black Chev would come to pick Debbie up. It was a black SUV. She didn't see the driver's face and assumed that it was Reg Law driving a different car. So maybe 'S' was driving the black SUV.

"We do know that, after hours, Debbie frequented Brewery Bay and may have met her killer there. The most important thing we have, is a thumbprint on the skin of Debbie's neck which was lifted off during the autopsy. We need to get a match for that. That could easily mean testing half of Mariposa and Coldwater."

"I guess we should start with the known suspects. Eliminate them first," said David.

"That's positively brilliant," said Clancy sarcastically, "I wouldn't have thought of that myself. How original. Got to search garbage bins, snap up beer glasses etc. If we think the killer is the driver 'S' who drives a black SUV, this might mean eliminating Harry Steppes. He drives a pick-up truck and rides a motorcycle I don't think he has the means to drive or own a black SUV unless the car is borrowed, but I think I should get his fingerprints just the same. I'll drive up there and fish around in his garbage to see what I can come up with. I'll go during Happy Hour when he's not around.

"Another suspect is Phil Short. I don't know too much about him, or what he drives. He hangs out at Brewery Bay. Chat him up and then try to get his beer glass. Switch glasses when he isn't looking. or trade your glass for his during conversation, making sure that you don't smudge the fingerprints."

"Will do."

"You're a wealth of ideas, David." Casey smiled. "Didn't know you had it in you."

Chapter 45

    Clancy continued chewing on his pen, picked it up then snapped it in two, then threw it in the waste-paper basket beside his desk. Everything in this murder case was a frustrating puzzle. Gary Potts, Debbie Love's boyfriend, is my most likely murder suspect he thought. If he found out Debbie was sleeping with other men, he has a motive, jealousy. The problem with that line of thinking, is that when I spoke to him, he claimed Debbie was virtuous, studying in the evenings during the week at Georgian College.
    This afternoon would be a good time to try to get Gary's fingerprints. If he's innocent, he'll have no objections. If he's guilty he'll make all kinds of excuses not to have them taken, thought Clancy. He drove over to the Y again, hoping to catch him there. Several young men with gym bags were rushing up the stairs, two steps at a time. A young woman in tight stretch pants passed by with a friendly "Hi, there." Obviously, she was saying that to the young man who followed him, not to an old goat like himself.
    Clancy showed the attendant his ID and went through the turnstile, then headed up the stairs to the second floor to the weight room where men with sweating bodies were groaning and grunting lifting bar bells and doing squats. He found Gary in a black track suit, facing a floor to ceiling mirror, bench pressing huge barbells. Seeing Clancy, he immediately put them down on the mat. then found a towel and wiped his brow.
    "You're a frequent visitor here. I don't like being interrupted. What brings you here again today? I told you all I know the last time you came."

"Would you have any objection to me taking your fingerprints? It's for the purpose of elimination. If you're innocent, it would prove that. We found a thumb print on Debbie Love's throat, a large thumb print, which we removed with a laser."

"No, I wouldn't mind, as long as I don't end up on the police data bank as a potential criminal and get stopped at the Buffalo or Windsor/US border for having a criminal record."

"Good. Let's go down to the snack bar. We can take them there."

Settled into a table in the corner under a poster that said, 'Carrot Juice is not just for rabbits.' Clancy pulled out a blue stamp pad. "It just takes a minute." He took one finger after another, pressing each into the ink and then onto a piece of paper. "Thanks for your cooperation, Gary. This is all I need from you at this time."

"How do I get this ink off?"

"Under a tap. Use soap and water."

"I want you to catch her killer as soon as possible, so that I can get on with my life. "

"We're doing the best we can."

Chapter 46

The afternoon was hot and sticky. Despite the rotor fan going overhead, Clancy felt the dampness on his shirt, under his arm pits. The heat was sapping his energy. It was time to stop and smell the roses. It was time for a cold drink.

Clancy headed over to Brewery Bay at Happy Hour to see if Phil Short was there. Going in along the crowded aisle at the bar, he spotted Mel Stone.

"A bit early isn't it for you? Lawyers work long hours, good for billing. I heard one lawyer even billed per minute for advice."

"The weather's nice, it's a warm day so I fancied a cold one."

"How's business?"

"Roaring. Real estate is booming. Houses are hot, especially properties around the lake. We're busy at the office. So busy I'll soon have to find another partner to replace Reg. I need someone to share the rent. Tell me, how is your investigation going? Any new developments, be sure and let me know."

"Not bad. Need to do some more digging. There are so few clues." Clancy watched while Mel put his empty glass down on the bar."

"Got to be going, but let's keep in touch." Mel headed out the door.

Clancy quickly grabbed the glass and put it in his canvas bag. Then he looked across the room to see if Phil Short had come in. He hadn't.

That can keep, thought Clancy, for another day.

Chapter 47

In the morning, Clancy phoned Harry Steppes to see if he was in. He let the phone ring and ring. No answer. He's out. That makes it a good time to call.

He drove up to Coldwater, phoned again to make sure he wasn't answering, then parked his car to the side of the house. He went up to the front door and rang the bell. Steppes' pickup truck and motorcycle were there. He must be in or maybe he'd gone for a walk. Harry didn't answer so he went around the back, to the black garbage bins that held the empty bottles and cans. He picked up some samples and put them in his bag. He'd just finished when Harry, still groggy from nursing a hangover, opened the front door and asked him what the hell was he up to. Startled, Clancy said, "I was just trying to find out if anyone was home. You hadn't answered the phone or the front door. So, I went around to the back. I wondered if you were alright."

"Sure. No, you weren't. You were snooping. Get off my property unless you have a search warrant, or I'll set the dog on you. Get off my property at once."

"Going, going, gone," said Clancy as he hurried to his car with the samples safe inside his backpack.

***

Clancy had tried unsuccessfully for several days to get hold of Phil Short

However, the next time he walked into Brewery Bay and looked along the back wall, there was Phil Short knocking back a few. This time he was in luck. "Ah, I thought I'd find you in here eventually. Your friend, Tony Gibbs. is going up before a judge in Barrie, on possession of stolen goods. You can arrange bail for him if you like. Just drive over to the courts in Barrie."

"Oh, fuck off. You know I don't have that kind of money."

"You have enough to drink in here."

"That's different. It's government money."

Clancy sat down on a chair besides him, "Mind if I join you? I'm thirsty."

"I do mind, but my hands are tied."

"Your hands are tied, my, my has it come to this?"

Phil Short gave him a dirty look. Clancy ignored him and called the waiter over. "I'll have what's he's having."

"Draught Labatt's Blue?" asked the waiter.

"Fine," said Clancy, "Here's to your good health." He quickly drank down to the level in the glass that Phil was at and nudged his glass closer to Phil's on the table. When Phil looked away at people coming into the bar, looking for some other companionship other than Clancy, he took the opportunity and switched the glasses. Thankfully, Phil didn't notice. There was a nice thumb print on the moist glass.

"I see someone at the bar that I meant to talk to," said Clancy. "See you around." When Phil looked towards the bar, Clancy slid the glass into his backpack then, getting up from the table walked towards the people leaning on the bar. He congratulated himself. Now, that wasn't too difficult was it?

Now to have the cans, bottles and glasses quickly sent to Forensics in Toronto for analysis.

Chapter 48

A banging on the office door. Clancy went to open it. Bob White was standing there.

"I thought I should drop over and catch up with how you're doing. Things have been busy and I haven't been able to get here."

Clancy beckoned him in and indicated a chair for him to sit down.

"The strangest thing happened to me last week," said White. "I kept hearing a rustling noise up in the attic over our bedroom. Later, outside on the back patio. I found a two-foot long boa constrictor curled up beside a potted plant. I nearly had a heart attack. I could have been strangled in my sleep. There's a bylaw against having or owning exotic animals.

"I phoned the Humane Society and it turned out that it belonged to my neighbor, who had reported it missing, a ditzy young woman who called the boa constrictor Pumpkin. She was a real flake. In the evenings she sat on the sofa with her snake in her lap, listening to classical music. Pumpkin loved it, she said. Skinny girl with nicotine stained fingers, ring in her nose. She rented the top floor of the house next door. Said she was a student at Lakehead University studying psychology. She kept repeating that Pumpkin was totally harmless.

"Well the bylaw states that owners can't own snakes over three feet long, so she didn't get fined. It had escaped its cage through a small space in the glass, then got outside and came up through the drainpipe to the attic, I could have been strangled in my sleep."

Clancy suppressed a smile.

"How is the investigation going?" asked White

"We're waiting for forensics in Toronto to evaluate some prints taken off beer bottles, pop cans and paper."

"That close, huh?"

"We might get a match."

"In that case, I'll be off. No need to stay."

"Sorry to see you go." Clancy held the door open for him and Bob White got back in his cruiser.

***

It was too early to go home.

"A call for you, Clancy. It's from Forensics, down in Toronto, with info on the thumbprints that you collected in the Debbie Love murder case.

Clancy picked up the phone and listened in excitement. They had a match. That was fabulous. The thumbprint found on Debbie's throat matched one collected off the beer bottles, not the paper he submitted nor the pop cans but the beer bottles. "Bingo," said Clancy," we've got our killer."

He put on his protective vest, packed his baton and hand-cuffs and picked up his gun, loaded it with cartridges, then slipped it into his holster and headed out. He drove over to Law and Stone office, but it was too late. A black SUV was pulling out of the lane-way at one side of the building. That's the car, thought Clancy with excitement, that's the kind of car I've been looking for. He decided to follow it, keeping one or two cars behind, well back from view.

When the SUV approached the railroad tracks Clancy slowed down. As luck would have it, he heard the clang, clang of the railroad signal and saw its flashing light. The wooden road barrier snapped down in front of him. A slow-moving freight train was inching its way through the crossing just as he got there. Rotten luck. Now he'll get away thought Clancy.

After the train passed through, Clancy pressed down on the accelerator. He raced ahead, the tire wheels spinning. The rubber was burning now.

Suddenly, an elderly farmer driving a tractor came out of the lane cutting him off. Clancy screeched to a halt.

Damn.

Finally, he saw the black SUV pausing at the next traffic light. Clancy pulled in slowly behind it. He followed, but on the next turn he lost the car completely. Then, a block away, there it was again. Thank gawd I haven't lost him.

If I get too close, he will try to lose me and then what? Clancy thought he was doing his best not to exceed the speed limits, but it was difficult. Sweat was pouring down his face. He tried to remain calm.

Again, the black SUV surged ahead. A horn blared. Then a cement truck slowly pulled in front of him, blocking Clancy's view and cutting him off. Clancy slammed on his brakes. The car skidded to a halt. Damn, thought Clancy, I'll lose him again.

'*Speed bump Ahead*', said the sign, but Clancy wasn't slowing down. His white knuckles gripped the steering wheel as his car hit the edge of it and the back end scraped against the pavement. A hubcap fell off. Forget it.

He could see potholes in the road ahead. The cruiser hit a big one. The car crunched and dipped, its springs bounced. A loud bang, then the side door of the car flew open. This rattletrap won't survive the ride he thought. He pressed his foot down on the accelerator and the car shot forward with the door slamming closed.

A construction worker held up a sign, '*Road under Construction, One lane only*'. Now Clancy had to wait for the oncoming traffic to file through, then it would be his turn to go. He could see the SUV ahead, exiting the lane. At least we're on a highway and there're not many turn-offs that he can take.

The black SUV headed north on Highway 11 in the direction of Port Severn, then made a sharp turn into the Riverhouse Restaurant parking lot. Clancy pulled in behind and.

As Mel Stone got out of his car, he looked around and was stunned to see Clancy walking towards him with his revolver drawn.

"You've been following me. What's up? What's with the gun? Are you out of your mind?"

"I'm arresting you for the murders of Reg Law and Debbie Love," said Clancy.

"Is this a joke? Some sick joke. You must be crazy. I'll sue you for every cent you have for false arrest. You're a hick cop from a small town. You won't have a job in this town when I'm finished with you."

"We'll see," said Clancy, "Your thumbprint was on a glass taken from Brewery Bay and sent to forensics to see if it matched the thumbprint found on Debbie Love's throat, the thumbprint you left behind on her skin when you choked her to death."

Mel's face flushed red. Angry, he yelled, "Don't be a fool. This is preposterous!"

"No this is justice. Justice for the murder of two people. Put your hands behind your back."

Mel suddenly jumped back into his car and started the engine backing up over Clancy's foot. Ignoring the pain, Clancy got off a shot, smashing the rear window. There was a shatter of glass. Another shot hit the engine. Oil dripped out onto the ground. Then he fired twice at the rear tires. Mel accelerated, and backed straight into the trunk of a thick tree. The wheels spun but the car would go no further. Clancy waited a few seconds and then slowly approached the car. Mel, with blood dripping down his forehead, sat in the driver's seat, too stunned to move.

"Come out with your hands up or I'll shoot." Mel's glazed, unfocused eyes didn't register a response. So, Clancy, gun drawn, dragged him out of the car, rolled him on the ground and snapped cuffs on him.

Suddenly there was an earth-shattering noise like a bomb going off. The car exploded. A whoosh of black smoke billowed up from the car. Then it was completely encased in flames. An angry, orange ball of fire shot up into the sky sending sparks everywhere. Some fell on Clancy's clothing, leaving small holes.

He had gotten that bastard out of his car in the nick of time or he would have been toast. He didn't know whether to feel happy or sorry that he'd saved Mel's life.

Clancy pushed Mel into the back seat of his cruiser where the doors lock automatically. Driving back to Mariposa there was a lot of thumping in the back seat, but Clancy was oblivious to it. He drove with a sense of purpose; he had gotten a killer off the street.

Chapter 49

David put a coffee down on Clancy's desk and brought his own coffee over. Next, he pulled up a chair. "Mind if I join you? I want to be brought up to speed on what's been going on. You've made an arrest in the Law, Love murder case. That's exciting news. What was the evidence?"

Just then there was a banging on the door. Clancy looked up and recognized Mrs. Proudfoot from the Mariposa Public library. Oh no, he thought, if she wants to sell me another raffle ticket I'm not buying.

"Yes, ma'am, what can I do for you. I'm very busy with cases that need to be solved. I can only give you a few minutes of my time."

She brushed that comment aside. "I have good news for you."

"Yeh, what is it?"

"You hold the winning ticket in our raffle. I wanted to come by and tell you in person. I made a special trip here to see you."

"What did I win?"

"A wonderful designer chocolate cake, delicious. You'll love it," exclaimed Mrs. Proudfoot. "You take your ticket over to the Mariposa Market and redeem it there. Your family will love it. Isn't that wonderful?" she gushed.

Clancy thought of his expanding waistline and sighed. "Thank you, very kind of you to come over here with the news. "

"Well, goodbye. You never know when you'll get lucky."

David tittered.

Clancy waited until she shut the door and then continued his explanation.

"The thumbprint matched the thumbprint on the throat and the one taken off the glass. Also, he drove a black SUV in which he took Debbie out on hook- ups. In her diary was the capital 'S' for Stone his last name. It's circumstantial evidence but I feel it's enough to convict.

"Nailed it, huh? So, tell me more." David took a sip of his coffee.

"This is what I figured. Debbie Love was a real hottie. She met her lovers in Brewery Bay at the bar after work during the week. She wasn't looking for sex as much as she was looking for money to help pay her rent and her expenses. In the law firm, she met up with Reg Law who provided cash. He treated her well, taking her out for dinner, etc.

"Debbie Love was very secretive, even her roommate didn't know what she was up to. Another reason was that I don't think her roommate would have approved of her being promiscuous.

"Then, Debbie added Mel Stone to her menagerie, picking him up in the Brewery Bay bar having recognized him from her temporary work at the law firm. After dating Debbie for several weeks, Mel found out that she was also dating Reg Law. Reg Law had foolishly confided in him over coffee that he was dating Debbie on the side, the implication was also that he was sleeping with her. Reg Law did not know that the other man in Debbie's life was Mel Stone.

"Mel must have gotten jealous and bitter about her treatment of him. He was not willing to share Debbie with Reg. I figured that he was the one who called her a whore in his phone call to her, the day before she was murdered. Earlier in the bar, I remembered him referring to her as a whore.

"To Mel, Debbie Love reminded him of his grasping ex-wife who had betrayed him and wiped him out financially. Debbie, too, wanted money from him and was also sleeping with his partner. Resentment and anger boiled over. He knew where they went, Reg had told him as much. He knew he took her to dinner at the Riverhouse Restaurant and, after parking near the locks, waited in his car in the parking lot and then followed them, keeping a discreet distance.

"Debbie had told him that she had a steady weekend boyfriend, but was not serious about him. He knew that the weekend boyfriend would be blamed, a perfect frame up for a perfect murder. But there were several inconsistencies, the angry phone call the day before Debbie was murdered calling her a whore, the letter 'S' found in her diary, the black SUV picking her up and the thumbprint on

Debbie's throat. Mel Stone was a smart man, but not that smart. He thought he had committed the perfect murders.

"Reg Law had tried to make a run for it when Mel broke the window of the car. Mel ran after him, hitting him on the head, then throwing his body into the lake."

"Now tell me, I'm curious. You told me that Reg Law was receiving threatening phone calls and he had told his partner about them. He figured on three possible callers and gave them to Mel. These names Mel gave to you. How do they figure in all this?" asked David.

"I finally figured out who was making the threatening phone calls to Reg Law. It was Mel himself. How hypocritical to pretend to be a friend, listening to Reg talk about his threatening phone calls and knowing full well that it was he who was making them.

"It was Mel Stone phoning Debbie at home. He used the landline at the office. So, tracing the calls wouldn't have helped. They could have been from Reg Law or Miss Neat. If he'd used his cell phone that would have been a different matter. The calls would have been traced to him alone," added Clancy.

"That's an interesting theory but we'll never know for sure. Anyhow you've got him behind bars, and he'll soon be up before a judge for a bail hearing, which they don't usually grant with first-degree murder charges." said David. "I'd heard that he was quite the man around town with the ladies, or at least he thought he was, flashing his money and expensive clothes in the bar to get whatever he wanted sexually. Not a nice man at all."

"That reminds me. I'll phone Mr. Love and tell him we got the murderer. It won't bring his daughter back, but maybe give him some closure, some peace of mind," said Clancy

He picked up the phone. Mrs. Love answered. ""That's good news. My husband is working in the barn clearing out the stalls. I'll go and get him. It'll take a few minutes."

He heard retreating footsteps and waited.

Mr. Love came on the line.

"Mr. Love. I have some important news to tell you. "Good news. We believe we've caught your daughter's killer. He's behind bars as we speak. The killer didn't get away with the murder of two people. He'll be going before a judge in Barrie. Bail will probably be denied. If convicted, he'll spend the rest of his life behind bars."

"It's good of you to phone me," said Mr. Love. "We've been wondering how the case was going. Not a day goes by that we don't miss our daughter. This won't bring her back, but we have some peace in knowing justice has been served. Thank you for telling us."

Clancy thought, as he put the phone down, that there was one more person to thank, Patty Blake. "David, I want you to go and thank Patty Blake. Tell her the news."

"With pleasure."

David picked up his jacket and headed over to her apartment. As luck would have it, Patty was sitting cross-legged on the lawn with her eyes shut, deep in meditation.

David strode up the walk. "Patty," he called out. "I have good news. Debbie Love's alleged killer is behind bars as we speak."

"Oh great, who is it? Somebody I know?"

"You might have bumped into him at Brewery Bay. His name is Mel Stone, he was a partner in Reg Law's law firm."

"Wow," said Patty. "No kidding."

"He was the one driving the black SUV and the 'S' in Debbie Love's diary."

"I can't believe it. Debbie was seeing three men in one week!"

"She was a busy gal."

"Her father would be horrified to find out, hence the secrecy surrounding her dates, He believed Debbie was virtuous," said Patty.

"I heard Mel Stone was quite the lad at the bar, chatting up the ladies for hook ups. Well, it will all come out at the trial. Thanks for your help."

"Thank you for coming over and telling me."

"Must go." David was reluctant to go, but he had to. Patty was a sweet girl. He wondered if she had a boy friend. Idle thinking. He got back into his car and drove back to the office.

Chapter 50

The next morning the sun was shining, the lake was calm, just the kind of day that puts a smile on your face, thought Clancy.

A light tap on the door, a pretty blonde-haired girl, with a ponytail, squeezed into the room. Leaning her elbows on his desk she asked. "Remember me? My name is Claire. My rabbit got stolen and I asked you to find it. I didn't get much help from you. I was very disappointed in your efforts to find him," she said.

"Well I have good news for you, I looked out the window this morning and found a large cardboard box sitting on our front lawn. When I lifted the box up, underneath was my rabbit. He wasn't harmed in any way. Someone had fed him and looked after him. So, you don't have to go looking for him anymore. The thief returned my rabbit."

"That's good news, Claire. I'll cross that one off my list. The file is now closed. Thank you for coming in and telling me."

Things are working out, thought Clancy, as he resettled himself in his chair after Claire had gone.

But his reverie was interrupted by the sound of heels clicking in the corridor. Mira blew open the door and flounced in, all bounce and jiggles, slapping her notepad down on the desk in front of him. Clancy mused the press were never far from the door.

Clancy leered at her, "Kiss any frogs lately, Mira?"

Taking off her black designer sunglasses and laying them down on his desk, she demanded, "Knock it off. MYOB. What have you got for me?"

"Plenty, Mira, plenty. I want to have good relationships with the press," said Clancy, trying not to stare at her plunging neckline, her breasts popping out.

"Yeh, well, one drink down at Brewery Bay is not good enough. You've picked my brains more than I've picked yours. Cheap should be your real name." said Mira, resentfully. "You owe me one. Cough up." And she flounced down on the chair in front of him, spreading her legs wide apart so he could see England, Scotland and France.

Clancy looked down at his feet, the only safe place to look.

"Big news. We've made an arrest in the killings of Reg Law, and Debbie Love. The man is in custody. You might know him. He's the real estate lawyer, Mel Stone. He'll probably be denied bail at the hearing to be held over in Barrie today. They won't release them on bail in the case of first-degree murder of two people. Right now, he's down the hall in his cell, screaming for justice. He's hired a high-profile lawyer from Toronto who's coming up today to throw his weight around. Money talks. Maybe you know Mel Stone, Mira? He was quite a player with the ladies at Brewery Bay."

"Yeh, I bumped into him the odd time at Brewery Bay. Snooty, not my type, he was full of himself. Thought he could get any woman in the room to put out with his expensive suits and fancy shoes that said 'money, honey'. I am not that big a fish."

"Thank goodness, Mira," said Clancy," you smelled something fishy otherwise you could have wound up with him and ended up dead. Speaking of frogs, I think I have a fair idea of the one who gave you a black eye and tore your blouse at the Round House, a while ago. In fact, I'll give you his address and you can go and check it out. Don't get too close, observe from a distance. See if it's the same person. If it is, come back and we'll press charges.

"He lives up in Coldwater, a twenty-minute drive from here. Has a motorcycle, lives alone. There's not much more that I can tell you. But check it out and get back to me."

"Will do." said Mira. "You've been very helpful, Clancy." She ran her red fingernail along his hairy forearm. "You're not usually this helpful, but we live and learn. Change doesn't happen overnight." Mira took the piece of paper with the address written on it and flounced out the door.

Chapter 51

With these murders solved, it was time to relax, Time to sit in the backyard, catch the warm rays of the sun and let the dog lick his bare toes. Clancy headed home. He found the lawn chair in the garage and pulled it out to the backyard. He took off his shoes and socks, rolled up his pant legs, lay down, closed his. He took a deep breath. There was nothing like fresh air. But his reverie was interrupted by the voice of Agnes yelling from the back door, "There you are, napping in midday, while the rest of the world is busy tidying up. The lawn needs cutting. There are weeds to be pulled, a thousand things need to be done around here."

"But Agnes, this is the first time I've had off since I solved the murders. This is my first time to relax."

"So," said Agnes raising an eyebrow, "no excuses."

"In a minute, Agnes. I'll do it in a minute."

"I should hope you do."

Clancy lay back thinking the office was more peaceful than this. He was in charge there. I'll lie here for twenty minutes then I'll go back into the office.

***

He was having a little nap back at the office when the door blew open with a bang. He shook himself awake. There was only one person who made such a grand racket, Mira.

"Mira, my favourite journalist, you have the look on your face of a cat that has been licking cream. What devilment have you been up to?"

With a grand gesture, Mira sat down on the chair in front of him, and slowly crossed her long legs. She paused dramatically and then gave him an electrifying smile. "Justice has been served."

"Hold on there, Mira, I don't like the sound of this. I don't want to hear of any vigilante stuff. Nothing done illegally. I have my job to protect."

"Let's put it this way, an eye for an eye, a tooth for a tooth, like in the Old Testament," she beamed.

"I've never known you as a Bible thumper. This is a surprise to me. You're not in Holy Orders." said Clancy. "Listen, you know what Gandhi would say to that, if everyone thought that way, the whole world would end up blind. Now tell me what you've been up to?"

"Well you tipped me off about Harry Steppes. I drove up there, early in the evening, just light enough to see him.

"I rang his doorbell and hid in the bushes by the side of the door until he came out. It was him alright. I recognized him straight away. No question about it. He stood there wondering who'd rung his bell. I swooped out of the bushes and gave him a knee to his jollies before he realized what had happened. When he was doubled over, clutching himself in pain, I gave him a swift karate chop to his nose," she smiled. "I heard a crack. I believe it might be busted. Then I took off. Has anyone called in to say that they've been assaulted? Probably not. Male pride and all," stated Mira.

"Mira, you did a dangerous thing, taking the law into your own hands. You should have phoned me and I would have arrested him for assault. You put yourself in harm's way."

"Justice was administered, short and snappy, no long drawn out court case of six months to a year or more, waiting for the judge to say something and then sentencing him to do so many hours of community service or twenty-four-hour home service. Most of the time they get off with a rap on the knuckles. People are not finding justice through the courts these days. In so many cases there's no closure. All the public gets is a big tax bill for court time. The victim gets nothing. No closure and no satisfaction."

"On the other hand, Mira," Clancy took a long pause to say this, He couldn't quite look her in the eye. "I could charge you with assault."

"Where's your witness? I told you all this confidentially." said Mira, giving him a hard stare and then, lowering her eyes whispering in his ear, "Do you want my help in future? I could be very helpful. On the other hand, I could do a lot of damage."

"Yes, Mira," sighed Clancy. "You've got me over a barrel. It was foolish to do that, very risky. He could have done you a lot of physical damage."

"I took my chances."

"You sure did. No flies on you, Mira. And you lived to tell the tale." Clancy sighed. "As Shakespeare said, all's well that ends well."